A BIG ANIMAL R[ ] THE SNOW.

He came from behind us. The strange sound I heard was his paws crunching the snow as he tore across the clearing. His eyes were on me!

The tingling that I felt on my back wasn't a tingle anymore. It was a chill that raced clear through me. It hit my legs and made me run. I only got a couple of paces when Mother bumped into me.

"Stop, Bub!" she ordered in her loudest hrronk. "Don't run! Stop! Stay behind me."

Mother turned to face the charging animal. . . .

Then I saw his eyes. They were brown, but the way he stared at me made them seem almost black. They made my heart pound in my ears.

He was after me!

Books by Bill Wallace

The Backward Bird Dog
Beauty
The Biggest Klutz in Fifth Grade
Blackwater Swamp
Buffalo Gal
The Christmas Spurs
Coyote Autumn
Danger in Quicksand Swamp
Danger on Panther Peak
A Dog Called Kitty
Eye of the Great Bear
Ferret in the Bedroom,
    Lizards in the Fridge
The Final Freedom
Journey into Terror
Never Say Quit
Red Dog
Skinny–Dipping at Monster Lake
Snot Stew
Totally Disgusting!
Trapped in Death Cave
True Friends
Upchuck and the Rotten Willy
Upchuck and the Rotten Willy:
    The Great Escape
Upchuck and the Rotten Willy:
    Running Wild
Watchdog and the Coyotes

**Books by Carol Wallace and
Bill Wallace**

The Flying Flea, Callie, and Me
That Furball Puppy and Me
Chomps, Flea, and Gray Cat
    (That's Me!)
Bub Moose
Bub, Snow, and the Burly Bear Scare
The Meanest Hound Around

Books by Nikki Wallace

Stubby and the Puppy Pack
Stubby and the Puppy Pack to
    the Rescue

Available from SIMON & SCHUSTER

Carol Wallace and Bill Wallace

Bub, Snow, and the Burly Bear Scare

Illustrated by John Steven Gurney

ALADDIN PAPERBACKS

New York   London   Toronto   Sydney   Singapore

First Aladdin Paperbacks edition October 2003

Text copyright © 2002 by Carol Wallace and Bill Wallace
Illustrations copyright © 2002 by John Steven Gurney

ALADDIN PAPERBACKS
An imprint of Simon & Schuster Children's Publishing Division
1230 Avenue of the Americas, New York, NY 10020

Also available in a Simon & Schuster Books for Young Readers
hardcover edition.
The text of this book was set in Trump Mediaeval.
The illustrations are rendered in pencil and wash.
Printed in the United States of America
2 4 6 8 10 9 7 5 3 1

The Library of Congress has cataloged the hardcover edition as follows:

Wallace, Carol, 1948-
Bub, Snow, and the Burly Bear scare / by Carol Wallace and Bill Wallace ;
illustrated by John Steven Gurney.
p. cm.
Summary: A young moose, his mother, and his animal friends team up to
fight a bully of a grizzly bear one long, hard winter, and make friends
with some humans in the process.
ISBN 0-7434-0638-9 (hc.)
[1. Moose—Fiction. 2. Forest animals—Fiction. 3. Bullies—Fiction.
4. Winter—Fiction. 5. Human-animal relationships—Fiction.]
I. Wallace, Bill, 1947- II. Gurney, John, ill. III. Title.
PZ7.W15475 Bu 2002
[Fic]—dc21   2001049040
ISBN 0-7434-0640-0 (Aladdin pbk.)

To
Linda and Neal Perrin

and to

Heidi Wilson
Laney & Hunter

Holly Byers
Brienna

Chapter 1

Tiny specks of ice filled the air and bit into my hide. Banks of white covered the mountain up to my knees. I followed carefully behind Mother, watching where each of her huge hooves left a print in the snow. It seemed as if we had been walking forever.

"Little Bub Moose, are you doing okay?" Mother's beautiful face peered back at me. Small icicles hung from her chin and her dewlap—the loose, flabby, beardlike piece of skin that swayed beneath her throat.

"I'm fine. Are we there yet?"

Mother rolled her big brown eyes. "You just asked that a moment ago, Bub. We're still not there."

A strange growly sound came from my tummy. I looked at the ground. There were no signs of tender morsels to eat.

"I'm hungry. Are we almost there?"

"No, Bub. We still have to move farther down the mountain. A stand of pines and aspens will mark the entrance to a valley where the snow isn't as thick. We should be able to find food there." Mother gave a low snort and began walking again.

It would be nice to get some warm milk from my mother. I was almost big enough to forage all on my own but not quite. I had learned many lessons in the forest and could take care of myself. But Mother couldn't stop to feed me. She needed all the strength that she had to keep us moving through the big snowstorm.

The sky darkened again. The wind whistled, driving the snow so thick that I could hardly see Mother's rump. Ice slapped against my face. We had stopped for a short time during the night. Now we had to keep going. Mother was determined to get us to the shelter of the canyon that she knew. My feet slipped as I tried to keep pace with Mother's long stride.

Alert for danger, I kept my ears perked. Mother had told me that we needed to be watchful for the wolves that were lurking in the trees. The only wolf that I knew was my friend Snow. We had gone on an adventure last fall when we were still babies. Actually, we had been lost together, but I really had a lot of fun with the little wolf.

It was hard to think that someone like Snow

3

could be a danger to me. Snow had helped me learn about things in the forest. When his parents found us, they didn't harm me in any way. They just wanted their baby back.

The forest was warm then. The leaves of the trees were just beginning to sprinkle down to the ground. We had played in them, hiding and jumping around for hours. The forest was very different now. Heavy snow covered everything. Small trees were shrouded in white. Some were totally buried by the heavy blanket of ice and snow.

The hungry feeling in my tummy kept coming back, but I knew that I must be brave for Mother. Someday I would be on my own. Being brave was probably a good lesson for me to learn. I could hear small grumbles coming from inside of me. Being brave was hard to remember when I was so hungry.

"Are we almost there?" I snorted for Mother.

"We may have to stop soon, Little Bub. It will take us another day or two before we reach the valley. We may have to rest." Mother's fur seemed to sag around her big bones. I suddenly noticed how tired she looked.

"It's okay, Mother. We can stop if you think we need to." I spread my long legs out to keep from slipping.

"That might be a good idea, Little Bub. Come, get some milk."

I scooted closer to Mother's warmth. When I

leaned down to get my milk, I could see a broken willow tree a few feet away. Probably snapped by the weight of the snow, the place where it split was bright and shiny. The light-colored wood reminded me of my friend Dudley. Only, he didn't break trees. He chewed them down. Mother's milk made me feel safe and happy. I closed my eyes.

I could almost see Dudley and the clearing where we first met. I had been just a baby back then. Mother told me that Dudley was a beaver and had lived in the forest for a long time. Asleep near a pile of brush where Mother had left me, I almost got whacked with a little tree Dudley took down. He was a nice beaver and managed to warn me to get away, just as the branches fell near my bed. Dudley worked all the time. The other beavers weren't nearly as busy as he was. Mother said that was why he got to stay at the pond. His children moved on to places of their own.

I couldn't help but wonder what Dudley was doing right now. Was he working, or was he safe in his beaver lodge with his family? Or was he . . .

"That's enough, Bub. I have to keep strong." Mother's voice snapped me from my daydream. She gently nudged me away. "I am going to lie down for just a bit."

Mothers legs slowly folded beneath her. I looked

around. It seemed safe enough, but Mother looked so weak. I stood over her listening for the sounds that meant danger.

It had been a long time since I had heard the wolves call in the distance. I listened for the special sound of Snow's little howl. Straining my ears, I only heard the wind rustle the trees nearby. Even the wolves must be hiding in safe places.

Mother's eyes were closed tight. White frozen powder swirled around us. Sometimes the icy crystals stung my eyes. Still I kept watch. Slowly I dropped to my knees, then curled up near Mother. I tucked my ears and listened only to the sounds of her breathing. A quick nap, then we would move on.

Heavy clumps of snow dropped from my lashes when I opened my eyes. I shook my head and glanced around. Mother was still asleep. I shoved my back against her belly. Small clouds came from her big nose. Pushing again, I moved her slightly.

"Mother, wake up. We have been asleep for a long time. We need to be moving on. It's getting dark." I stood and stared down at her.

"Bub Moose. I am so tired. Have we been here very long?" Mother asked.

"Long enough to get covered with snow and ice. We need to get going. I am hungry, and we have to get to the valley you told me about. I don't think it is ever going to quit snowing." I nudged Mother with my nose.

Struggling, she got to her feet. Shaking snow and ice from her body, Mother stuck her big nose into the air and snorted.

"You're right, Little Bub. We must keep moving. Come on."

Mother's strides were shorter than before. It was easier to keep up with her. I even bumped into her rear a time or two.

"Bub, move ahead of me. Just keep walking along the mountainside until you see some trees. We need a shelter where we can spend the night."

Mother let me lead. My hooves broke through the icy snowpack. Taking steps cautiously, I watched for the trees. Mother let out short snorts to let me know that we were on the right trail.

We followed along a ledge that was sheltered by the mountain. The little bit of light was beginning to fade. Being the leader made me feel very grown-up and brave. Until . . .

A strange tingling feeling raced down my spine. It kind of prickled the hair at the back of my neck— just behind my ears. It was a weird feeling, like someone or something was watching. I looked all around. There was nothing but Mother. She was farther back than she was a moment ago. I slowed my pace as we moved on. But the strange tingling that made my ears twitch just wouldn't go away.

A dark silhouette at the top of the mountain peak suddenly caught my attention. Like Mother had taught me, I stopped dead in my tracks. Sharp eyes focused, trying to make out what it was. I stood staring for a long time. I didn't blink. I didn't even breathe deep.

"What is it, Mother?" I whispered.

Mother didn't say anything.

"It's so dark I can't tell what I'm looking at. Do you see it?"

Again there was no answer. I turned to see if she was watching the same thing I was.

Panic filled my heart.

"Mother? Mother, where are you?" She was gone.

I forgot about the animal I thought I saw in the distance. Eyes wide, I perked my ears toward the spot where I had last seen Mother. Instead of her huge brown frame and her long beautiful nose, there was nothing. Behind me, the white emptiness of the falling snow was all I could see. I spun around so quickly I almost buried my hind legs in the deep soft powder. I lunged and yanked myself free.

I had to find her. What if she had fallen? What if she was hurt? I had to find her, fast!

"Hrronk . . . hrronk! Mother where are you?" My legs trembled as I charged back down the path.

I felt so very alone.

Chapter 2

"**H**rronk, hrronk!" I trumpeted as loud as I could. My eyes searched the path as I hurried down the mountainside. Only one set of hoofprints had come this way. Mother hadn't followed me.

"Hrronk, hrronk! Where are you?" I perked my ears listening for any familiar sound.

"Bub Moose, stop with the hrronking. You'll start an avalanche. I was just coming to get you. You got off the path. Come this way. There is a stand of trees down there. It's not much shelter, but it should protect us a little from the storm."

Relief filled the pit of my stomach when I heard the sound of Mother's voice. At the same time, the part of me that had been so brave and grown-up was suddenly replaced with fear. I would have to take care of myself soon, but I couldn't even follow a simple path to safety. How could I be on my own when I wasn't nearly as grown-up as I thought?

"Down here. Step carefully. The path is covered with ice. Don't slip."

I eased closer to Mother's side. I rubbed against her. As the sky began to darken, I felt tired and afraid. I never wanted to leave Mother. Maybe I could stay with her forever.

"Watch out, Bub Moose. It is a long way to fall if you aren't careful. Keep your eyes sharp and watch my steps. We're almost there." Mother nudged me slightly and I took my place behind her.

The small stand of fir trees didn't offer much shelter from the driving snow. It did break the wind a bit. Beneath two trees we found a small pile of brush to nestle behind. Walking in circles, Mother tromped the limbs flat with her big hooves. When she was finally satisfied with our bed, she nestled down and motioned for me to come and curl up beside her.

The fir trees blocked the wind—but not much. Mostly it was Mother who kept me warm. I loved Mother so, so much. It wasn't long before I dozed off.

I don't know what pulled me back from my sleep. There was a deep covering of snow on me that was helping to keep me warm. But my back—where Mother was—that was very, very cold. Using my hooves and legs, I pushed back to snuggle tighter against her. Only I didn't feel her warmth.

My eyes sprang wide. I snapped my head around to see where she'd gone. When I saw Mother wasn't there, I raised up from the snow and scrambled to my feet.

Mother stood about three strides up the mountain. She seemed to be frozen, with her head high and her nose to the wind. Her nostrils flared as puffs of steam came from them.

"Mother? What is it?" I whispered in my softest hrronk.

She didn't answer.

"Mother?"

"Something is there," she whispered back, without turning to glance at me. "Something's watching us."

I stared into the darkness. The snow swirled thick and heavy.

"What is it, Mother?"

"Something." That was all she said.

"I saw something, too," I told her.

"Where?"

"When we were walking. Before I came back to you."

"Do you know what it was?"

I shook my head. "No. It was on the crest of the mountain. The snow was very thick and it was almost dark. At first I wasn't even sure I saw anything."

"What do you *think* you saw?" Her eyes never left the dark hillside.

"I don't know. For a second I thought it was my friend Snow. It was about the same size. Only it had a flat nose instead of a pointed one. And its tail was really long and skinny, instead of fluffy like Snow's tail."

"A long, skinny tail?" Mother asked.

"Yes. Do you know what it is?"

Mother didn't answer. She stood for a long time. Her ears moved, first one direction then the other, picking up each little sound that might drift her way through the dark. Her nostrils flared and puffed, smelling for the slightest scent of danger. Her big shoulders were tense. Her muscles tight and ready.

"It sounds like Roscoe," she answered finally.

My head tilted to one side. "What's a Roscoe?"

Mother stomped a hind foot and turned to watch in a different direction.

"Roscoe is not a what, he's a who. Roscoe is a mountain lion. Two days ago I thought I smelled a scent that he left to mark his territory. I thought he lived around here, but I wasn't sure."

"Are mountain lions dangerous?"

Mother shrugged her ears. "Not to moose. They are usually smart enough to leave us alone, unless we're sick or hurt. But . . ." She raised her nose to the wind again. "But," she went on, "it has been a very bad winter."

I sniffed the air. I couldn't smell anything. I stared where Mother was looking. I couldn't see anything. Finally she gave a little sigh and glanced back at me.

"Lie down, Bub. There's nothing to worry about. You need to get your sleep."

"Are you going to snuggle with me, Mother?"

She smiled and gave a little toss of her head. "No. I'm not very tired. I think I'll sleep standing up tonight."

The next morning we climbed back to the path and went on our way. Mother still seemed tense. She led the way and kept glancing back over her shoulder at me and the path behind us. Then she let me lead for a while. If we came to a sharp turn in the trail that she couldn't see around, she shoved in front of me and led the way.

At a spot near the very top of the mountain, Mother stopped and sniffed the ground. Then her head snapped up, and once again she bent and sniffed.

"Yep. It's Roscoe. We should be out of his territory by this evening. Let's keep moving."

"What's a territory, Mother?"

"Mountain lions have a territory or area of land where they live. They think they own a whole lot. Sometimes a hundred and fifty to two hundred miles of the mountains, they call their hunting range."

"Hunting range?"

"They are meat eaters, Bub. But like I said last night, they usually don't bother moose. Now, let's keep going. We'll be away from him by dark."

Watching carefully because of the ice and snow, we walked down a steep slope, then up another mountain. Then we went down that mountain and up another. The snow wasn't nearly as thick and mean as it was last night. We stopped near a bunch of aspen trees to forage in the snow. There wasn't much to eat, so we didn't stay long. When the sun was high in the sky, the snow picked up once more. The wind blew the snow and whistled as it whipped up the mountain slope where we walked. I ducked my head against the sting of the little bits of ice.

All at once I snapped up my head. That tingly feeling came crawling up my spine once more. It made my ears perk and twitch.

There was nothing there. Nothing but that creepy feeling.

It was about dark when we came down into a wide valley. The snow was heavy and deep, but the wind was not nearly as strong as it had been higher up.

"Is this it, Mother? Is this the valley? Are we there?"

"Not yet," she answered. "We will probably reach our valley tomorrow. But this is a good place to spend the night."

We wandered into a clearing. Mother spotted a big pile of brush that would block the wind. We had just started toward it when I heard this strange crunching sound. I glanced over my shoulder.

A big animal raced across the snow. He came from behind us. The strange sound I heard was his paws crunching the snow as he tore across the clearing. His eyes were on me!

The tingling that I felt on my back wasn't a tingle anymore. It was a chill that raced clear through me. It hit my legs and made me run. I only got a couple of paces when Mother bumped into me.

"Stop, Bub!" She ordered in her loudest hrronk. "Don't run! Stop! Stay behind me."

Mother turned to face the charging animal. He had a flat nose and little pointy ears. His tail was long and skinny as could be. It kind of spun around behind him as he bounded through the snow. His long legs seemed to gobble up the ground as he raced toward us.

Then I saw his eyes. They were brown, but the way he stared at me made them seem almost black. They made my heart pound in my ears.

He was after me!

I wanted to run so bad I could hardly stand it. It was all I could do to stay there, behind Mother, like she told me.

I never felt so scared.

Chapter 3

The mountain lion raced closer and closer. His sharp teeth glistened against the black edges of his mouth. Any second I expected him to leap and . . .

At the last moment he stopped. Snow piled up in front of his paws as he slid to a halt. Arching his back, he turned sideways and hissed.

Mother lowered her head and lunged. She didn't really charge, though. She took one mighty lunge, then stopped. The mountain lion dodged to the side.

"I'm hungry," he snarled. "That little moose looks just the right size."

I started to run.

"Stop!" Mother ordered. "Stay behind me."

The mountain lion circled us. Back arched and each step quiet and soft, he moved closer and closer.

"I don't want to hurt you. Just get out of the way so

I can get at the kid. I'll leave you alone, I promise."

Mother snorted at him. He took another step. Suddenly she reared up on her hind legs. When she came down, her front hooves swung out and pounded at him. He dodged out of the way. Her hooves almost shook the ground when they hit. Roscoe hissed and raised a paw. Circling again, he flipped his tail and started back toward us.

"You cannot have my baby," Mother snorted. "You're old enough to know not to mess with a moose. What's wrong with you?"

Roscoe kind of sucked in his tummy. "I'm starving. I haven't had a rat or a rabbit in almost a week. I'm hungry."

"We're hungry, too." Mother snorted. "But you can't have my baby."

"We'll see about that."

Mother pawed at him once more. Snarling, he leaped aside.

"I don't want to hurt you," she said. "But if I have to, I will. Then you won't be able to hunt. *Then* you *will* starve."

The mountain lion kept circling—kept inching closer to us. As Mother circled with him, I moved, too, so I would stay behind her like she told me.

"Let's talk this over," Mother said. "Surely there is someplace else you can find a meal."

"No way." Roscoe sighed. "I've looked everywhere. There's not so much as a mouse. With all this snow, if I don't find something to eat pretty soon, I'm going to . . ."

Mother didn't let him finish what he was saying. In the blink of an eye she reared up and bounded toward him on her hind legs. Her front hooves clawed the air. I heard the loud thud when one caught the big cat on his left shoulder. He let out a weird squeaking noise and scampered away.

I expected Mother to back up to where she had left me. She didn't.

I raced to get behind her. She sprang up on her hind legs and kept slashing at him with her mighty hooves. Roscoe snarled and growled. Each time she pawed, he scampered and scooted and dodged to get out of her way. Mother chased him almost to the edge of the clearing before she stopped.

As soon as Roscoe got the chance, he spun around and raced back up the side of the mountain. Far enough away and safe, he slowed down. When he did, he limped a bit—favoring his left side.

Mother gave one last snort at him, then we trotted back to the brush pile.

There she kissed me and cleaned me with her long tongue.

"Mountain lions are cats," Mother said. "Don't ever run from a cat or a wolf. They chase you if you run."

"But he wanted to eat me!"

"I know." Mother kissed me again. "But don't

ever run from a cat. If you stay and fight . . . well, even if you're a little moose . . . you have a chance. If you run . . ." Mother kissed me once more. "Don't ever run."

Mother slept standing on her feet again that night. We left early the next morning. Even after a good night's sleep, I felt so tired I could hardly stand. We walked and walked and climbed and climbed. We went uphill and downhill and then up again. I thought we never would reach the valley. The snow came harder and faster. The wind blew. Now it was almost like a blizzard. I didn't know if I could go on. I just wanted to curl up in the snow and sleep . . . forever.

It was nearly dark on our third day of traveling when we came to a stand of trees. There were five pine trees, and just below them was a stand of aspen.

As we made our way farther down the steep slope, I noticed that it seemed a little warmer. The wind wasn't as wild and cold. The snow didn't seem to be as deep, either. The fierce storm swirled above us instead of jabbing its cold icy fingers into our faces.

"Are we there yet?"

I could see Mother nod her big, beautiful head.

"We're there. This is our valley."

If I hadn't been so exhausted, I would have hopped

and leaped and bounded with joy. As it was, I just kept walking.

Mother suddenly stopped in her tracks. I perked my ears and tried to look into the darkness. Shadows trailed across the ridge, but I couldn't see anything.

"What is it, Mother?" I whispered.

Mother stood stiff and proud. "Hush! Just a minute, Little Bub."

I tried to stand as tall as Mother. I kept my head pointed in the same direction as hers. I didn't see anything.

"Is it Roscoe? Did he follow us, Mother?"

She shook her head.

"No." She sighed. "Roscoe learned his lesson yesterday. Besides, he won't come this far out of his territory. Roscoe won't bother us here."

"Then what is it, Mother?"

"It's worse than a mountain lion," she whispered. "There are people here."

"I don't see anything. How do you know that there are people here?" I pawed at the snow with my hoof.

"Come in front of me and look, Bub. There are buildings that weren't here the last time. There is a wood fence and a wire fence that were not here before."

Squinting, I blinked a couple of times. The valley was wide. It was dark and the snow, even though not blowing and swirling, was thick. It was hard to see. Slowly shapes began to form. I thought one of the things was a cabin, but I wasn't sure. (Snow and I saw lots of cabins and buildings once, when we were lost in the people town.) This shape was sort of like a cabin . . . only . . . there was another shape behind it. A building maybe. No, a barn. (Snow and I met a cow once who lived in a barn.) Still not quite sure what I was looking at, I sniffed the air and took a step closer.

"Stay back, Bub Moose. We don't know where the people are. With the storm, they are probably inside keeping warm. But with people—you never know. They're strange animals. We'll sleep in the safety of the trees now. When morning comes, there will be enough light for you to see. Perhaps the storm will be over by then."

We found a little clearing that was well hidden in some trees. We foraged some, but just barely found enough food to nibble. My tummy felt better, but I hoped that tomorrow, when the sun came up, we could find more. I was very hungry, and I knew that my mother was, too.

The darkness took the storm. The snow fell gently now. It was no longer blowing and biting. Mother trampled a bed for us next to a pile of brush. When she lay down, I knelt near her and nestled against her big warm body.

I looked for the shimmering stars in the sky. The

clouds that brought the snow were still too thick. The only light that I could see was across the valley where Mother said the house was. Brightness, like big stars, shone from the place where she said the people were. I watched and listened for a long time. I felt warm and safe, next to Mother. Slowly I drifted off.

Chapter 4

When the light from morning finally began to creep into the valley, everything was crisp and white. Pine limbs drooped beneath the heavy white covering. No snow was falling. The storm was over. I blinked away the sleepiness. Mother was still curled up near me. We were both covered with a blanket of glistening powder.

Gently I shoved against Mother. She didn't wake up or look at me. She only tucked her face down even lower. I guess she needed a little more sleep.

Carefully I pulled myself up on all fours. I shook the white from my back, my wobbly legs braced as I shivered in the clear, crisp morning air. Since Mother was still resting so peacefully, I decided to take a little walk before I woke her. She seemed really nervous about the new people buildings that weren't here the last time she came. I needed to check them out. If there was danger, I could hurry back and warn her. Then we could run away. But if it was safe, I needed to know that, too. Mother would feel much better if she didn't have to worry so.

The sky was just getting pink as I started off. At the edge of the trees I stopped. The high mountain valley seemed even bigger than it had last night. Of course, it had been really hard to see—what with the darkness and the thick swirling snow still falling. Beyond the valley was a ridge. It was not as high or steep as the one we came down, but it protected the valley from the driving blizzards that Mother told me always came in the winter.

Near the center of the valley, but a little closer to the far side, there was a people cabin. It was bigger than most of the ones that Snow and I had seen in the town, the time we were lost there.

A heavy blanket of white lay between me and the cabin. Cautiously I stepped into the clearing for a better look. Most of the cabins Snow and I saw on our adventure were small and covered with flat, white boards. This one was like the little hunting cabins in the forests, except that it was much larger. The sides were made of round logs, stacked one above the other. A little trail of smoke came from a pile of rock at the very top.

There were other buildings near the big cabin. I

still couldn't see very well, so I moved closer. One step at a time I eased out into the clearing between me and the people place. The only sound was the crunching of the snow beneath my feet. At the center of the open area I stopped. It made me feel a little nervous. Moose are much happier and feel safer when there are trees or rocks to hide us. But from here I could see almost everything.

To my left the valley seemed to stretch for miles up toward the high country. There were trees and a flat area where there was maybe a pond or something. Beyond that a creek or stream with steep banks. Everywhere, the snow was white and smooth as could be. No animal tracks broke the surface. No other living thing had been here—nothing had touched this new snow—except for me.

A bright golden glow replaced the pink of the sky. I could see much better. Behind the big log house was another building. It was almost as large, but instead of being covered with logs, it was covered with flat red boards. It was a barn. A fence, made of logs, came out from one side. Beyond that was another, made of wire. This fence surrounded a big pasture. Between the barn and the cabin was a smaller building. And at the back . . .

A sound made my eyes flash and my head turn. I blinked and held my breath.

It was a growl. Soft and tiny, it sounded like the growl Snow used when he was trying to frighten all the children away at the school. I tilted my head to the side and wobbled my ears. Louder now, the sound moved toward me.

"Hrronk!" I whispered softly. "Who's there?"

There was no answer, but the growly sound got louder. Closer. I didn't like it—not one little bit.

Fear made the hair on my legs tingle. Turning, I strolled quickly back toward the trees. Exploring would be better when Mother was around.

Before I made it there, the growly sound had grown to a roar. I raced across the meadow and hid behind a huge pine. Rumbling like thunder, the sound moved closer and closer to the people cabin. I peeked through the pine needles. Snow sprayed into the air in great clouds. It flowed up and up, only to fall once more. When it came down the snow made a hill. I couldn't figure it out. Snow fell from the sky. It didn't fall from the ground into the air and then back again. This didn't make any sense.

Then . . . suddenly . . . I saw it!

A huge monster rumbled toward the people cabin. Black smoke belched up from the top of its head. Enormous round teeth spun in its mouth as it gobbled up everything in its path. Snow spewed high into the air.

My eyes grew wide. My legs trembled.

Then . . . something thumped my bottom.

Attacked from the rear, I didn't take time to turn around. I just jumped . . .

Right into the pine tree.

I was never so happy to see Mother's long, beautiful face in my life. She seemed to be a bit startled at first. Then she wobbled her head, snorted, and gave me a rather disgusted look.

"Bub, get down from there. Moose don't climb trees."

"I-I didn't know you were there," I stammered. "When you nudged me, I thought there was another monster and he was going to gobble me up."

Mother tilted her head to the side. "Monster?"

"Yes. Like the one who's going to eat the people cabin. See?" I pointed to the clearing with my nose.

Mother squinted. Then she sighed.

"That's not a monster, Bub. It's a snowblower. A people machine. It clears the snow away." I guess she could tell from the look on my face that I didn't understand. "Remember the roads where the people cars go?" she asked.

"Yes."

"Well, the people cars can't go in the snow. Their legs are round and short, not long and strong like ours. If they try to go through snow, their tummies drag and they get stuck. So the snowblower machine has to come along and clear the snow away from their roads."

"You mean there's a road there?"

"Yes. It's hidden by the deep snow. When the machine leaves, I will show you. Now, get down out of that tree before you hurt yourself."

Having never been in a tree, I wasn't quite sure how I was supposed to get down. In fact, I wasn't quite sure how I got up. There was a limb under my tummy, right in front of my hind legs. There was another limb under my chest, right behind my front legs. My hooves dangled. I kicked my feet and twisted and flopped around. Next thing I knew, the branch under my chest bent and my front end slipped off.

Only my back end under my tummy was still stuck on the branch. My front feet barely touched the ground. I stretched, but I just couldn't quite reach. So here I was, with my rump in the air and my head and front feet dangling above the snow.

"Bub, quit fooling around. Get down from there right now."

"I'm trying, Mother. Honest."

I kicked one hind leg, then the other. I kicked again and again, until it felt like I was running— upside down. Finally the limb under my tummy gave a little crack, and I fell.

Struggling to my feet, I fought my way through the limbs and bounded to Mother's side. She let me get a quick breakfast of milk, then we moved back into the stand of aspen to forage. Using her long nose and lips, Mother scooted the snow aside and found some green twigs to chew. Now and then she would rear up on her hind legs and nibble on fir boughs. I chewed some of the green twigs, too. They weren't very tasty.

As we moved along the side of the mountain, I kept looking back over my shoulder. The snow-blower was going the other direction, now. I could see the dark, shiny road behind it. On either side there were high mounds where the machine had thrown the snow. White plumes shot into the sky, but the roar from the machine was almost gone.

As Mother foraged farther up the valley, I held back just a little. I was curious to see the rest of the people place. Surely Mother wouldn't mind. Learning about new things and exploring is what young moose are supposed to do. Besides, I didn't sense any danger. Something inside told me that, with the snow monster gone, I was perfectly safe.

I headed back across the clearing, toward the cabin. The ridge of snow beside the road was like a little mountain. It was steep and slippery. I made it to the top, then slid down the other side. Once across the hard, black road, I dug my hooves in and climbed the second snowbank. At the top I stopped. Listening, I strained to hear any sounds that I didn't recognize.

Clunk!

My ears shot straight up. I froze. Held my breath. Keen eyes spotted two things moving toward the pen at the side of the barn.

People!

Chapter 5

I think they were people. People sort of looked like that. I had seen some, close up, when I was lost with Snow. The sounds that they made sounded like people noises. They were covered with fur, but not like Mother's and mine. The people that I had seen weren't shaped like this, either.

These were round and roly-poly. Only their eyes peeked out from under their coverings. These things didn't really walk on two legs, like people did. They sort of waddled. Their fur was so thick they could hardly move.

"I wish Mother wouldn't put all this stuff on us. I can't even walk. I feel like if I fall over, I'll be stuck like a turtle on its back. All I'd be able to do is flop around and roll back and forth. I'd never be able to get up with all these layers of clothes on."

"Oh, quit complaining, Jane. We're running late as it is. I don't have time to listen to you gripe about having too many clothes on. Get some grain for Raney and Sweet Pea. I'll get the hay. Maybe, if we hurry, we can go look over the ridge to see if they are skiing yet." The taller one headed to the barn.

"Wait up, my legs don't work very well in all this stuff."

"Mother thought it was icy out here. She wants you covered up all over. It doesn't feel very cold in all of this stuff, but your skin can freeze pretty fast if it's exposed to the wind. Just hurry so we can see if the resort is open."

I couldn't quite see them as well as I wanted. There were two small fir trees nearer to them, but I would have to go through the open area to get there. I looked all around. Listened. Then I darted across the clearing and hid behind one of the trees so I could watch. The two round people opened a door and moved out of sight. I tried to see what could be inside the big building. Outside, the snow was really bright. Inside, all I could see was darkness. I stretched my neck and peered at the spot where the people had been.

The tall one came out carrying something that looked like grass, but it was green. This time of year all the grass beneath the snow was brown. The little person had something in each hand. They walked away from the barn.

I had to move from my safe place to see where they were going. Quickly I darted behind the second tree. The people waddled to a wooden fence. Two big animals were inside the pen. My ears perked when I heard small whinny sounds as the people opened a gate.

"Jane, go around to the side and pour the grain in their buckets. They're watching me, and you can get out of the way before they go after the oats."

"You'd better hurry yourself," the little short one said. "Raney acts like she hasn't eaten for a week."

The smaller round people climbed up on one of the logs and poured something into a bucket that was tied to the fence. The other one tossed the pile of green grass on the ground in front of the big animals. I hadn't seen animals like these before. They looked a lot like Mother. They had beautiful long brown noses. They were tall like Mother, but their ears were small and pointed.

"Come on, Jussy. You said we could go look at the ski resort." The one called Jane set her buckets on the ground and wobbled toward an open space behind the pens.

"Okay, but we have to hurry. It's almost time to go to school. I heard the snowplow when it went by this morning. The bus won't be late today."

The round pudgy people wobbled off toward the ridge on the far side of the valley. I glanced around for Mother. She must still be foraging.

When I got to the fence, I had to lean down so I could look between the big logs to see the large animals better. These things were huge. They were about the size of Father. Maybe even a little bit bigger. They had their heads down foraging inside the pen.

"*Snort!*"

I jumped back. One of the animals was looking right at me. Suddenly I didn't feel very brave anymore.

"What are you?"

"I'm Bub Moose!" I tried to sound as big and strong as I could. "We came from another valley. My . . . my mother and I are looking for food. What . . . what are you?"

"They call me Raney and this is Sweet Pea. We work here. We pull a big sleigh. They call us draft horses."

"I saw a cow once. You kind of look like her."

"A *cow!*" Sweet Pea exclaimed. "Like . . . whatever are you thinking? Cows are . . . like, stupid. We aren't stupid. We are strong and beautiful. I came from California. You know, *the Valley*. The Valley is the coolest place. Like, there are people everywhere and shops, and . . ."

The other horse gave a little snort.

"I thought you told me the Valley was warm." She frowned at Sweet Pea over the top of the feed bucket.

Sweet Pea glanced at her and fluttered her eyes. "Like, really. In summer it's totally hot."

Raney stopped munching her food. "But just now you said the Valley was cool."

Sweet Pea's head flopped over to one side. "Okay, we took people on hayrides in a big wagon. They talked and sang songs and there was always something to do. So . . . that was cool. But . . . well . . . like, it's cold here and warm there. And—well, it's like a different kind of cool. Okay?"

The horse shrugged her ears and stuck her head back in the bucket. Sweet Pea sighed and winked at me. "Sorry. Sometimes I get like totally carried away. Raney is from Indiana. We were picked because we are totally awesome. We aren't stupid like cows, are we, Raney?"

"Uh, I don't know. I really don't know many cows." Raney bit into the grassy food in front of her.

"What are you eating? It looks really good." I moved a little closer to the fence.

"Duh . . . it's hay. We get hay and oats two times a day. Do you want some? There is enough for you."

"I'd better not. Mother would be mad at me. She may be mad anyway 'cause I'm not where I'm supposed to be." Sniffing the ground, I moved just a bit closer to the pen. It did smell delicious.

"Go get your mama. We have bunches and bunches. They always bring us PL . . . EN . . . TY!"

"I . . . I . . . I don't know. It smells wonderful.

But . . ." I stretched my nose between the logs of the fence, then quickly pulled back.

"Tell you what, Little Sweetie. We'll save enough for you and your mama. You can bring her around anytime, and there will be some here for you. We have oats and sweet feed to finish up with. That's our favorite. *You do* need to get your Mama down here and eat the hay before they bring us more this evening. Our people won't give us food if there is still some lying around." Raney tossed her head and trotted to the bucket on the fence.

"That would be great. Mother will be proud of me for finding her some food to eat." I stepped back just a little from the fence. "Thank you."

"You are . . . totally . . . welcome. We'll share with you . . . like . . . anytime." Sweet Pea turned away from her hay and headed to the other bucket.

A chill raced between my shoulders. I perked my ears and listened. The two people were coming back toward the pen. Frightened, I hurried to the shadows of the fir tree near the barn.

"Hey, look at that. It looks like a pony. But *what* is it, Jussy?"

"Be quiet, Jane. You'll scare it. I think it's a baby moose. We have to be really careful. If its mother thinks that we are going to harm it, we could be in real trouble."

The people stopped near the bottom of the hill and just stood there for a long time. Finally they moved slowly until they were near the big log cabin. Standing as still and motionless as the fir tree, I watched them. I never closed my eyes. I didn't even blink. After a while they quietly turned and disappeared into the building.

The people made me a bit nervous. I glanced back at Raney and Sweet Pea. Still eating from the buckets on the fence, they didn't seem the least bit worried. Surely there was no reason for Mother to be afraid to come and eat. Suddenly both of the horses perked their ears and looked toward the snow-covered meadow. I heard it just then, too.

"HRR-ONK! HRR-ONK! Bub Moose, where are you?" I saw Mother near the road in front of the cabin. She was calling as loud as she could.

Instantly my feet took me running toward her. Adventure time was over. I had to tell Mother about the horses that I had met. She would be happy to know that they would share their food. Mother would be soooo excited.

Chapter 6

"**H**RRONK! Bub Moose!" Mother trumpeted louder than I had ever heard before.

Lunging and bounding, I raced toward the sound of her voice. There was something different about her call. Something scared or hurt or . . . I charged faster through the soft white powder. The sun peeked above the ridge behind the people cabin. Even at my back the bright sunshine made the snow so shiny that it almost hurt my eyes. Squinting, I tried to find Mother. It was hard to see, but I finally spotted her. Long neck stretched up toward the sky, she called me again. What if she was hurt?

"Mother! What's wrong? I'm coming." I galloped toward the place where she stood. My hooves dug into the snow as I bounded across the clearing and charged up a tiny rise.

Then . . .

The snow was gone. My hooves dug into nothing but air. My eyes flashed. My heart leaped into my throat. I was falling.

I guess I kind of forgot about the two steep ridges of snow that the big people machine had left. When I topped the little rise, I remembered. Only it was too late to stop. There was nothing below but the black shiny road—and it was way, *way* down there. My front legs stretched out and went stiff. I couldn't stop. When I finally touched the snow, I slid for a ways. But instead of slowing down, I only went faster and faster.

Then I lost it.

Next thing I knew I was on my back in the middle of the hard, black road and the whole world was kind of spinning and wobbling around me.

"Bub! Do not play in the road!"

"Huh? What?"

Mother stood at the crest of the other snowbank above me. Looking very stern, she glared down.

"Children don't play in the road. It's too danger-ous. Get out of there, right now!"

I got about halfway to her when my hooves slipped out from under me. My legs crossed as I tried to catch my balance. At the bottom of the hill I was on my rump with my legs in a tangled mess.

"Hrronk!" I squeaked.

"Bub Moose, I mean it. You get up here, right this instant!"

I unscrambled my legs and hopped to my feet. When I finally made it to the top and to Mother's side, I bumped her with my nose to let her know I wanted some milk. She squirmed to the side and shoved me away with her big hoof.

"You can eat in a moment. First, I want to know where you have been. I searched all over. I couldn't find you."

"I . . . ah . . . er . . . I slipped when I jumped over that pile of snow and I fell. I really wasn't playing in the road."

Mother's look was stern. "Before the road. Where were you?"

"I . . . was . . . ah . . . exploring. Yeah, that's it. I was exploring the valley. I got an idea. Why don't we go up that way? I bet there are some really good places to forage and—"

"Don't change the subject. Where have you been? I have been looking for you. When we forage, you are supposed to stay close enough to see me at all times. You certainly haven't seen me for a *long* while!" Mother's eyes didn't look soft and sweet as she stared at me.

"What's wrong. Are you hurt? I heard you calling for me, but these mountains of snow are in the way. I was hurrying to get to you." I tucked my head a little.

"Bub, you are doing it again. Where were you?" Mother stared straight at me.

"I . . . I . . . I met some new friends."

"Not people!" Mother looked shocked.

"No." I shook my head. "They were horses. *Really big* horses. They live behind the log building. Raney came from Indiana. Is that like a different part of our forest?"

Mother didn't answer. She just looked at me.

"And Sweet Pea came from the Valley," I went on. "Only, she didn't say which valley. She talks kind of funny, but they're both really nice. Honest. They said they were draft horses and they pull a wagon and a sleigh and they have food and they want us to come and share it with them. Sweet Pea told me to get you. She said that there was plenty for us." I shook my head and tried to straighten my fur.

"You were near the people cabin, weren't you?"

"Well, not really. Well . . . ah . . . sort of."

"I told you that there are people here. You can't be too careful with them around. Come on, we have to get away from this place." Mother shoved at my rear.

"But, Mother, you don't understand. There is a big pile of food for us. All we have to do is go eat it. Sweet Pea and Raney are saving it just for us. They said that we need to get it before the people come back with more, or they won't leave them any. We have to help them eat it up." I stood firm in my tracks.

"Little Bub Moose. *You* don't understand. Those

horses belong to the people. They depend on them to bring food. We don't belong to anyone. We are on our own, and we have to take care of ourselves. Now, come on. We have to move away before more people come and see us."

"I saw the people. They didn't look dangerous. They were kind of round and roly-poly. I don't think they would hurt us."

"Bub Moose, did they see you?" Mother stared down at me.

"Uh . . . I don't think so. I mean no. No one saw me," I lied. Well, it wasn't a big lie—just a little one.

"We have to go. People will be moving around, now that the storm is over." Mother nudged me again.

"But there is plenty of food. It smells really good. I'm hungry."

"Let's go, Bub Moose." Mother kissed my cheek with her long, rough tongue.

Head low, I followed close behind her as we trudged up the valley. My stomach felt grumbly, but I knew that I better listen to Mother. We just made it to the edge of the trees when all at once Mother turned her big head and perked her ears. She looked back to where we had been. I stretched out my legs and stared in the same direction. A loud roar came toward us. Standing perfectly still, I searched the wide space in front of me. I finally spotted something moving toward the buildings where the people lived.

"Stay very still, Little Bub Moose. It's a bus coming for the children in the cabin." Mother barely moved to breathe.

A huge yellow car barreled down the road and stopped near the building that we had been so close to. The two roly-poly people waddled quickly toward it. I didn't blink as I watched to see what would happen next.

Just before they got to the enormous yellow car, one of the people started pointing at me. I stepped back a bit. The person raised a front leg and began shaking it back and forth. Loud sounds came from inside the big yellow car, but I wasn't sure what I heard.

The two pudgy people disappeared through the opening. The clamor started again, and then it roared away.

"What was that about, Bub?" Mother turned her head to the side and stared at me with one eye. It wasn't a soft brown eye, either.

"Wh-what?" I mumbled.

"That girl. She waved at you. You said that no one had seen you." Mother lowered her head, and the one angry eye looked straight into me.

"I . . . I don't know. Maybe she was happy to see *you*! I don't know." Head down and holding my breath, I started foraging for food once more. Behind me I heard Mother give a little snort.

I followed close, just as I was supposed to. Except

for dry twigs, there wasn't much to eat in the trees. We wandered farther up the valley, toward the high country. Every now and then I could hear Mother's tummy rumble. I bet if we had shared the hay Raney and Sweet Pea offered, she would be full and happy. I didn't say anything, though.

Once away from the people place and the road and the big yellow bus, we left the shelter of the trees and moved into the clearing. There, beneath the snow, we found some dry grass to nibble. I used my hooves to scratch at the snow on the ground. We moved farther and farther away from the buildings and the people. We foraged for hours.

Why wouldn't Mother believe that it was safe to eat the hay? Why wouldn't she listen to me? I bet Raney and Sweet Pea could convince her that it was okay. If only she would talk to them, I bet . . .

I suddenly noticed that Mother had stopped hunting for food. She stood still as a rock, with her head high and her ears perked. She was holding her breath.

Listening, I froze, too.

"I don't hear anything but my stomach growling." I whispered, feeling tired and hungry.

"Hush. Listen to the sounds in the trees." Mother wobbled her ears toward a spot just ahead of us.

"Where? I don't hear anything." I tried to focus all of my attention on where she was staring. My stomach growled. It was so loud that I couldn't even think about the sounds, much less hear anything.

"I recognize those noises. I just haven't heard them in the wintertime. This isn't the right time to hear these sounds," Mother said.

I watched the trees. Suddenly my ears caught the sound that she had heard. I had heard it before, too.

Clunking and rustling noises were just beyond the edge of the forest. I glanced up at Mother. She stepped closer to the safety of the trees. Nervous and jittery, I followed her. My hooves were ready to run back to the buildings if I needed to. Mother was afraid of the people. For some reason, I felt safer with the people than I did here.

"*Crunch, crunch. Gnaw. Scrape. Gnaw.*" The noises grew louder.

"Is that Dudley?" I whispered.

Mother shushed me.

"Can't believe it," a strange distant voice mumbled. "Work and slave all spring and summer—clear into the fall—and this is what I get. Cut trees until my front teeth are down to the nubs. Drag the things across the valley. Work my tail to the bone. And this—this is the thanks I get."

There were more crunching and gnawing sounds.

"It wasn't my fault. I didn't even know old Burly was within miles of that tree. I didn't mean to." There was a long sigh. "Rotten luck. That's all. Now I'm stuck out here in the freezing cold. I can't even feel my feet anymore. Can't believe it. Just can't believe it!"

Chapter 7

"Look, Mother. It's Dudley."

We stared at the beaver as he sat on a mound of tree limbs that poked out of the snow.

"I don't think that's Dudley. Dudley's tucked safely in his lodge back at his *own* pond." Frowning, Mother tilted her head to one side. "Besides, beavers don't work during the winter. They stay in their lodges because their ponds are frozen. Why would a beaver be working in this cold?" Mother shrugged and turned away to forage under the trees.

"I can't believe that this keeps happening to me! Just about the time I get things fixed up, crash, boom, I have to start all over again." The beaver glared down at the top of the mound in the pond.

I studied him for a moment. Buckteeth. Big flat

tail. That just had to be Dudley. Slowly I ambled from the safety of the trees for a closer look.

"Hello. Is that you, Dudley?" I called out.

Balancing on his tail and hind legs, the beaver sat up and looked around.

"What? Who's there?"

"Hey, Dudley. Remember me? What are you doing here?"

Ice cracked when I stepped in the snow at the edge of the pond. His little ears perked, and he squinted toward me.

"Get back, kid. Are you trying to wreck things more than they already are? I can't take it." The beaver stood at the edge of the mound and shook his front paw at me.

"Don't you remember me? I'm Bub Moose. You helped give me my name. Don't you recognize me?" Giving him my best profile, I looked up toward the sky.

"Hey, kid, what do you think? I'm not Dudley. Dudley is my dad. He's back at the big pond with all the little squirts. He never had bad luck like this. He has the perfect home. Nobody ever comes around there busting up his place." With a sigh, he picked up a limb in his teeth and stuck it on top of the mound. "Just about the time I get this thing fixed so I can relax a little, here he comes, charging out of nowhere, to tear it up."

"If you're not Dudley, then who are you? You look just like him." I stared.

"You can call me Chippy. If you know my dad, then you are a long way from home. I got booted out of his pond when the last kits came. I walked forever to find a place that wasn't already loaded with beavers." The beaver picked the limb back up, turned it just a little, then stuck it back in the mound.

"My mother and I just came here. We are looking for a good place to forage. The big storm covered up all the food. Do you know of any good places to eat?"

"You've got to be joking. I don't have time to eat. Don't have time to sleep. If I so much as close my eyes, here he comes, crashing through the trees, smashing everything in sight. First time he tore up my beaver dam. Just barely got it put back together before the freeze. If I hadn't had water around my lodge . . ." He turned and tapped the limb down with his tail. "Mostly he tears up my lodge."

"Is that what you're working on?"

"Yeah. This makes the second time he's ripped the top off my house. Got to fix it or I'll freeze to death. I'm so discouraged. I may have to go back home. I can just hear my dad now. 'What are you doing back home? Didn't I teach you to take care of yourself?'"

"I'll bet Dudley will be happy to see you."

"You must be talking about another Dudley."
Chippy sighed, shaking his head. "My dad doesn't
want any of us to come back after we have left the
pond. He says that it means he didn't do a good job,
if we can't take care of ourselves. For Dudley, it
would be another mouth to feed. There are two sets
of babies still living there now. I've got to figure this
out on my own. If he comes back again . . . Oh,
my!" The beaver scampered out into the snow and
picked up another stick.

"You keep talking about *he*. Who's *he*?"

Chippy put the limb on his lodge and went after
another.

"*He* is Burly."

"What's a Burly?"

"It's not a what, it's a who. Burly is his name. He's
a grizzly bear. One big, mean, nasty old grizzly
bear."

"Do you know why he keeps tearing up your
home?" I asked.

"Well . . . you see . . . it was just sort of a little
misunderstanding. That bear has *no* sense of
humor." Chippy started arranging the branches on
top of the mound. He stood back, studied them a
moment, and tapped them into place.

"What kind of misunderstanding? Maybe you can
talk to him and get things straightened out." I
watched as he paced back and forth, picking up
twigs to bring back to the pile.

"What are you, some kind of psychologist?" he said when he got the last twig to the lodge. "That bear won't listen to anything. I tried to apologize. He just won't listen. I said that I was sorry. Sorry, sorry, sorry! He won't slow down long enough to hear a single thing I have to say."

"What did you do that you tried to apologize for?" (Maybe this was more complicated than I first thought.)

"Well . . . I was just starting out. I hadn't cut down very many trees. I did really fine when I was working with my dad. But . . . ah . . . when I tried on my own . . . ya' see, I did okay with little trees." Chippy started pacing back and forth on top of the lodge. He paced faster and faster.

"You did fine with little trees. So?" I coaxed.

"So . . ." The beaver sighed and stopped his pacing for an instant. "It shouldn't have made him that mad. He wasn't really hurt or anything."

"What happened?" I asked.

"Okay, but don't tell my dad. I don't think he would be very happy to know that a grizzly bear is chasing his son." Chippy plopped down on the lodge.

"I won't tell anybody. Well, maybe my mother, but she won't tell your dad, either."

"Okay, it's like this. I had just moved away from home. Found this neat valley, here with a great stream. Perfect place to build my dam. I was working on a good-size tree . . . *big* tree . . . I couldn't see around it. How was I supposed to know he was wad-dling by. It really wasn't my fault. I mean . . . any other bear would have had sense enough to move. Not Burly. *Whaaap!* It sort of fell on him. Didn't hurt him. Sure did make him mad, though. He charged after me. I ran! Just barely made it into the water where I was safe. We can move flat out in the water. No way a bear can get around fast enough to catch us, once we're in a pond. But he splashed in and tore up everything I'd done. Now and then I'd pop my head above the surface and tell him that I was sorry. Didn't make a bit of difference—not to Burly."

"When did you see him last?" Mother asked as she walked up to us.

"He tore the top off my lodge this morning. I'd move—you know, to a new valley—but it's winter. All the ponds are frozen. I have never known any-body to hold a grudge like this. Besides, I thought bears were sleeping this time of the year. Aren't they supposed to hibernate for the winter?" Chippy looked straight at us.

"You did say his name was Burly?"

He clicked his buckteeth and nodded. Mother rolled her eyes and shook her head.

"I've never met him, but I have heard about him." Mother stood next to me at the edge of the pond. "Story goes that people built the ski resort right on top of his den. With all the racket going on, he developed insomnia. Been a terrible grouch ever since."

Chippy and I looked at Mother, then at each other, then back at Mother.

"What's insomnia?" we asked at the same time. Then we glanced at each other and giggled.

"He can't sleep," Mother answered. "You're right, Chippy—bears *are* supposed to hibernate this time of year. They curl up and sleep all winter long. Burly can't get to sleep. That's probably what makes him so cranky."

"I'm so depressed. I should have had my home built a long time ago. It's gonna be spring, and I will still be packing mud. Florence is getting fed up, too. She'll probably leave me."

"Who's Florence?" I asked.

Chippy pointed toward the lodge with his buck-teeth.

"Florence is my wife."

"Why isn't she helping you fix your lodge?"

"She says that she's not the one who hit Burly with the tree. I did." Chippy sighed. "Besides, she's in what's left of the lodge—pouting."

His head drooped. "If only I'd watched when I chewed that tree down . . ."

"Don't be so hard on yourself," Mother soothed. She leaned forward and gave him a gentle nudge with her long, beautiful nose. "From what I've heard about him, Old Burly is mad at *everything*. You could have dropped a leaf on him and he would have been mad. He could be upset because it is snowing. Nasty tempered as he is, he'll find someone else to be mad at before too long. He'll forget all about you and leave you alone."

"If I live that long," he sighed.

"Cheer up, Chippy," Mother said. "Just hang in there. He has to go to sleep sometime. Maybe he'll find a new den. When he wakes up, he'll be in a better mood."

The beaver started to work on his lodge once more as Mother and I moved back toward the trees. Behind us, I could hear him mumbling: "Just my luck—drop a tree on an insomniac grizzly bear. How depressing . . ."

"I feel sorry for him," I whispered to Mother.

"Me, too." She nodded. "He is very depressed." I guess she noticed when I frowned and tilted my head to one side that I didn't understand. "*Depressed* means that he's sad. Unhappy," she explained.

I followed close at Mother's heels. We strolled back down the valley. My tummy growled. "Are we going to share some of the hay with Raney and Sweet Pea now? Is that where we're going?"

"No, dear." Mother shook her head. "We need to be alert with Burly around. Bears don't like people. Moose don't like them, either, but we should be safer down closer to the cabins. Only, not that close."

"But, Mother. I'm so hungry and . . ."

Mother nestled next to me in the pile of brush where we spent last night. I fell asleep listening to my tummy growl.

Chapter 8

Wiggling and twisting most of the night, I just couldn't get settled. My tummy rattled and growled. I tried to stay as quiet and still as I could, hoping that would help me go back to sleep. When the sky finally started to turn pink I pulled myself up and shook off the night.

Looking back to make sure Mother was still asleep, I started for the barn. Maybe there was a little bit of hay.

There were no people near the cabin. There were no cars, snowblowers, or big yellow buses rumbling around. Quietly and quickly I trotted into the clearing, crossed the road, and stopped near the fence where Raney and Sweet Pea lived. At first I didn't see them. When I walked a little farther, I spotted them standing under a small shed with their backs to me. Just like Raney had promised, there was still hay piled near the fence.

I slipped closer. The yummy green stuff was just out of my reach. Dropping to my knees, I stuck my head between the logs and stretched my neck as far as I could. My lips quivered as I took the sweet hay into my mouth. I nibbled and crunched the wonderful-tasting food. Pulling my head back, I got to my feet. Mother should be awake by now. Raney and Sweet Pea didn't mind sharing their hay. Mother needed to eat and this hay was so good and . . .

Suddenly the fur on the back of my neck felt prickly, as if something was watching me. It was the same feeling I had when Roscoe was hunting me. But Mother said Roscoe wouldn't bother us here. She said we were safe from him. Then I remembered Chippy and Mother talking about Burly. What if *he* was watching me? Mother said that moose don't like bears. Moving nothing but my eyes, I stood perfectly still and looked around.

The girl leaned against the logs at the edge of the cabin. She didn't move.

I stared at her. She stared at me.

There was something familiar and safe about her. I could feel no sense of danger as I watched her eyes. We stood for a long long time. Finally I turned and started away from the pen where Raney and Sweet Pea lived. The little girl didn't chase me. She just stood and watched.

Mother was munching some dry grass when I got back to the aspens where our bed was. She lifted her head and perked her ears when she saw me trotting toward her.

"Bub, where have you been?"

I ducked my head.

"I'm sorry, Mother. I was really hungry, so I went to get some of the hay that Raney and Sweet Pea left. The little people girl saw me. I should have been more watchful. If I hadn't gotten caught, there would be some hay left for you, too. Now the people won't leave extra hay. It's all my fault. I'm sorry."

Mother gave a little snort. "Don't worry about it, Bub. We don't need the people food. We are going to visit a new valley today. Be sure that you keep me in view all the time. With Burly around I don't want you very far away. You are getting big and strong, but we need to save our strength for finding food rather than fighting off a grumpy old bear."

"I'll stay close."

We moved slowly up the valley, stopping now and then to forage. There wasn't much food to find beneath the snow. The sun was high overhead as we started climbing a long slope toward another peak. Just as I was pulling myself up the last ridge, Mother stopped in front of me. I eased beside her so I could see why she stopped.

"Wait, Bub! There are people here." Mother

looked long and hard at the snow in front of us.

Staring, I tried to see what Mother was talking about. When I finally spotted the people, my ears shot straight and my eyes popped wide. These people were way up on the mountain slope to our left. At first they were not much more than tiny dots. But as they zoomed toward us, they got bigger and bigger.

Mother had shown me the cars that people moved in. They went really fast! These people didn't have cars around them. Still . . . I couldn't believe how quickly they streaked down the snow toward us.

"What is it, Mother? How do they move so fast?"

"The people animals call it skiing. There are smooth pieces of trees attached to their feet. The wood helps them slide on the snow. They do this for fun. See, down near the bottom of the hill." She twitched her ear to the right. "When they get there, they slow down. They even stop and take the wood off." She leaned to the side and bumped me with her nose. "Up here we have to be very careful, though. Some of the people are wild and dangerous. They're crazy and go so fast they can't stop."

I watched as the people appeared from the trees and moved down the slope.

They whizzed this way and that. Their voices filled the air with happy sounds and laughter as they called back and forth. Powder poofed from beneath them if they turned sharply. When they zoomed

past, right in front of where Mother and I hid, my eyes blinked and almost crossed inside my head.

I couldn't believe it. People only have two legs. Moose have four. But even with four legs, I could never move that fast.

Cautiously I stepped away from the trees. Maybe if I could see up the hill, I could get a better look at the skiers and . . .

Whoosh!

Something zoomed right in front of me.

Swisssh!

Another something zipped right behind my heels. Whatever it was, it went so fast I didn't have time to see anything but a blur. I yanked my neck around to see what and where it went. Two skiers left strange tracks behind them as they sped down the hill. One turned to look back at me.

"Did you see the moose?" he screamed.

When the other one turned to look back, they crashed into each other. All at once there was a big explosion of snow. Then I could see pieces of wood and legs and arms and everything. It was a big ball all tangled up and rolling around in the snow in one big floppy, churning pile, and . . .

"Bub! Get over here right now!" Mother snorted. "You're going to get run over if you stay out there on the slope. Let's go back to our valley."

Mother didn't have to tell me twice. The people noises—their laughter and giggles and yells—made the skiing stuff sound like *fun*. Even so, it was weird. I was ready to go.

The sun was already hiding behind the mountain when we finally got back to our valley. Mother sniffed and snorted as we neared the pile of brush where we slept. She held her big head high and looked all around.

There, near the edge of the trees, were two big piles of hay. Mother and I stood perfectly still, for a long, long, long-long time. Finally certain that there were no people around, we moved to the soft green hay and sniffed. It smelled *so* delicious. My lips quivered as I reached for a bite.

Mother stood watch while I ate. When I finished, I stood watch while she filled up on the luscious, wonderful green hay.

That night, for the first time since the heavy snows started, I didn't hear my tummy growl when I fell asleep.

When I awoke the next morning, I listened for the grumbly sounds from inside. I couldn't hear them. I felt full and comfortable. Closing my eyes, I could almost taste the sweet, delicious hay that we ate last night. Mother's tummy didn't growl, either. She got up and stretched.

"Come on, Bub. Time to get up and hunt for our breakfast."

I stood beside her, yawned, and tried to shake the

sleep off. All at once my eyes flashed wide.

"Look, Mother. Over there where the hay was yesterday. There's more. It came back!"

Mother made me wait at her side, until we saw the yellow bus rumble down the road. As soon as the little people got inside the thing and left, Mother and I eased out from the trees and went to eat the wonderful hay.

The next morning, it was the same thing, and the next and the next.

Then—one morning—the big yellow bus didn't come. Mother and I waited and waited. The sun was high above the mountain peak when we finally spotted the two short people waddling toward us from the barn. Carrying two piles of the fresh green stuff, they dropped it in the snow. The little girl waved at me. They stood there a moment, then trudged back toward the house. The next day, the little boy and the little girl came again. But the third morning, when we woke up, the hay was there waiting for us. The big yellow bus came, too.

Over the next few weeks we learned that the big yellow bus came at the same time, day after day. But then for two days it didn't come . . . but then it did. It was confusing, but we finally learned the pattern.

On the two days that the bus didn't come, the little people waited until late in the morning before they brought the food for us. Mother, always more alert and watchful than I, told me that the man people was the one who usually brought the hay. She said he woke much earlier than the little people, and that's why the hay was always waiting when I got up.

I learned a lot about the people animals during those weeks. I learned that the little girl was named Jane. She always called the little boy Jussy. But when the mother people called them to come inside, she called him Justin. Mother always called me Bub, and I was curious why the boy people had two names. I learned that on their front legs they didn't have hooves—they had what Mother called hands. They could pick things up and hold them. They could make little balls out of the snow and throw them at each other. They could even pick their noses with them, if they wanted to.

I also learned that Jane and Jussy were not as round and plump as I thought.

One day the sun was very bright. The air warmed so much that drops of water began to fall from the clumps of snow that made the pine boughs droop. Jane and Jussy waddled from the house and began playing in the snow. They made a round ball with their hands, then they dropped it and pushed it along. The ball grew and grew. Before long the little white ball was the size of a big rock. Panting and wiping their faces, they stopped.

My eyes flashed wide when Jane and Jussy took their fur off and dropped it. I eased closer to the edge of the trees so I could see. I lost some fur, one time, when I brushed against a jagged tree limb. It hurt. Jane and Jussy didn't even seem to notice. They strained and grunted as they tumbled the ball of snow. Now it was as big as a boulder. Again they stopped and took off more of their fur. When the ball was so big they couldn't move it, they rolled another ball. Smaller than the first one, they lifted it and put it on top. Then they rolled a third and heaved it up.

The mother people—I guess her name was Mama because that was what both of them called her— yelled for them to come inside. They picked their fur up off the ground and disappeared into the log building.

Once they were gone, Mother and I felt it was safe to eat. We just finished when Jane and Jussy scampered back outside. Quickly Mother and I galloped to the safety of the trees. Again, the two little people were covered with fur—all round and roly-poly. That afternoon, when we came back from foraging on the mountainside, the pile of snow looked like a people. Well, it sort of looked like a people. It had sticks for arms and a long orange, pointy nose. Its two eyes were made of something black, and something bright and fluttery was wrapped around its neck. It was weird.

Chapter 9

One morning I slept in. I felt so warm and cozy that I just didn't want to get up. Lying there for a while, I noticed this strange feeling creep over me. I tried to lift my head to see if our food was in the clearing yet. Only my head wouldn't move. Now I felt *really* strange. It was like something was holding me. I blinked and opened my eyes. I couldn't see!

Startled and scared both, I sprang to my feet.

Okay . . . I didn't spring. I struggled and jerked and squirmed. Finally I gave a mighty lunge and stood up. It was unbelievable. There was snow everywhere. Deep new powder covered the entire world. I glanced back at my bed. There was nothing there but a round hole with snow piled at the edges. No wonder I felt so strange. I was buried.

"Mother, do you see this? I can't believe it. I've never seen so much snow. Mother? Mother?"

There was a crunching sound beside me. Soft white powder flew into the air as Mother's head popped through the crust.

Startled, I jumped back. Only my hind feet were buried deeper than I thought. So . . . I jumped back with my front feet and my back feet just stuck in the snow. I ended up, sitting down, smack-dab on my bottom.

Mother looked at me and blinked a couple of times. I blinked back at her.

I started giggling at the sight in front of me. Mother looked so funny. All I could see was her big beautiful face and head. Her large ears flipped at the snow that covered them.

"You look pretty funny yourself, Little Bub," Mother said.

I glanced around at my rear end. My bottom was buried in the big pile of white powder. When I wiggled my short tail, snow flew around in swirls. After easing my back legs free, I stood on the big pile of snow and shook from my head to my rump.

"Let's go. I'm hungry," I begged Mother.

"I want to stay here just a little longer, Bub. This snow cover is warm and comfortable."

"But . . . I'm starving!" I begged.

"Bub Moose, you can go on ahead and look for the hay. Watch for the people, though. I haven't heard the bus this morning. I want to rest just a little bit longer. I'll be there in a while."

"I'll watch for the people. I'll be careful." I felt big and almost grown-up because Mother trusted me to go look for the hay pile by myself. Listening and watching, I marched proudly to the spot where the hay usually was. It wasn't there. Scratching the snow with my big hooves, I tried to find a bite that we had missed yesterday. There wasn't even a flake of hay. My tummy growled. My ears drooped.

In the distance I could see the two big horses standing with their heads over the fence. They weren't eating, either. I crossed the open pasture and the road.

"Hey, Bub," Raney called when I strolled up to their pen. "They haven't brought the hay out yet. The big snow has caused them to be late."

Sweet Pea whinnied and nodded her head.

"Well, yeah, they're late because of the snow. It's like Christmas vacation, too. And . . . you know . . . like, kids get a kick out of sleeping late during vacations."

My head leaned way to one side. "They get kicked? Vacation?"

"Jane and Justin don't have to go to school today," Raney explained. "They like to sleep late."

"We don't get Christmas vacation." Sweet Pea curled her top lip way back. "It's vacation for the people, but a total drag for us. Man, like, we do two hay rides every day. More people show up at the ski resort. We work twice as hard. For them, it's party-time."

My mouth fell open. I turned to Raney. She shrugged her ears, as if to say that she had no idea what Sweet Pea was talking about, either.

A loud noise near the house made my head snap around. Jane and Jussy waddled toward the barn. Though I had watched them a lot from the safety of the trees, I had never been this close before. My feet seemed to freeze to the ground as I stared at them. If I didn't move, maybe they wouldn't see me. I watched as they went into the barn, then came out carrying piles of that delicious hay.

A soft growl came to my ears as my tummy began to talk to me. I couldn't move. I just stood there staring at the delicious food.

"Look, Jane," Jussy whispered. "It's the baby moose."

Under the bright orange fur that covered her head, Jane's little mouth curled up on both sides. Her eyes got almost as big as mine. "Come here, little Moosie. We have some breakfast for you."

Flicking my ears, I looked around for Mother. Jane and Jussy looked bigger than I thought. Jussy stopped, but Jane moved a bit closer.

"Little Moosie, come here. This is for you." Jane dropped the hay, then squatted down in the snow close to it.

I took a small step. I let out a little warning snort to let her know that I wasn't afraid. Dropping my head, I put my nose into the hay. Jane sat very, very still while I ate for a while. Finally—ever so slowly—she eased to her knees and leaned toward me. I stopped munching the hay, but I didn't move. She leaned closer.

"It's okay, baby Moosie. I won't hurt you. I promise." Jane's voice was gentle and sweet.

I looked into the little people's eyes. They twinkled as bright as the white snow. There was no mean or evil in her look. I could sense no danger. Lifting my head ever so slightly, I took a step closer.

Kneeling on the ground, Jane was shorter than I was. Slow as a fall leaf fluttering to the ground, she reached out a hoof (I mean, hand). I watched as it moved toward my head. Her eyes were bright and warm. I blinked and licked my lips. Not quite as slow or cautious, I leaned forward. Jane let out a little giggle as she touched the fur behind my ear.

At first her touch felt strange. It made me just a little nervous. But the more she rubbed and scratched behind my ears, the better it felt. Jussy scooted up on his knees. He reached out and stroked my neck. That didn't feel too bad, either.

Then I saw the mother people. She stood a little ways from us. I could see the tracks in the snow, behind her, but she wasn't coming toward us. She seemed almost frozen—tall and as stiff as a pine tree. Her face was stern and worried, only she wasn't looking at us. Glancing over my shoulder, I saw Mother at the edge of the trees. Her face was worried, too. She watched us, then she looked at the people mother, then she watched us again.

"Jane. Justin." The mother people's soft voice didn't seem to go with the tense look on her face. "Both of you stop petting the moose. I want you to back away—very slowly."

Justin scooted back on his knees. Jane didn't follow. She giggled again and stroked my long ear. I flipped it. Justin reached forward and tugged at her fur. "Jane. Something's wrong. You'd better mind Mama."

"But the little moosie is so sweet. Can't we—"

"Jane!" The mother's growl was soft as a whisper. "Right this minute!"

The little girl blinked her eyes at me and smiled. I blinked back and waved with my ears as she scooted off. Once away from me, both of them got to their feet. Justin latched on to the fur at the back of her neck. Watching my mother, over his shoulder, he made Jane walk with him as they moved slowly back toward the house.

Mother's nostrils flared. Steam puffed from them like the clouds of white that puffed from the snowblower. "Bub Moose," she hrronked. "Do not run. If you run, they might chase you. Turn very slowly and *walk* to me."

"But, Mother. They were nice. They weren't trying to hurt me. And—"

"*Bub Moose! Now!*"

As loud and angry as Mother's voice was, it was hard for me to walk. I wanted to run. Only, there was something about her tone that made me do what she told me to. The mother people did not turn when Jane and Jussy reached her. Walking backward, she eased away from us.

Once they were at the cabin, the mother was not happy.

"You're eight years old," she scolded Jane. "You know better than to get that close to a moose. They are very dangerous animals and—"

"But, Mama. The baby moose was sweet. He liked me petting behind his ears and—"

"You didn't even see the mother moose, did you? Do you know what would have happened if she thought you were hurting her baby? Do you have any idea what would have happened to you two if she had charged . . . ?" The mother stopped and turned to Justin. She shook her finger right under his nose. "And you, young man. You're in fifth grade. You're supposed to take care of your little sister. If I ever . . ." Her voice faded as they moved inside the people cabin.

Smiling, I trotted up beside Mother and leaned down for some milk. She moved away from me. Steam still puffed from her flared nostrils. I moved again and reached for some breakfast. Mother spun. She lowered her head and butted me on the bottom. It was not a friendly or an affectionate butt, either. It hurt.

"I have warned you about getting near the people," she scolded. "I've told you how dangerous they are. And what do you do?"

"The little people are sweet, Mother. They were nice to me. I think they want to be friends."

Mother butted me again. "You can't be friends with people. They are far too dangerous. If I ever catch you that near to them again . . ." She let out a snort and butted me one more time.

As we walked up the valley to forage, I tried to tell Mother about the people. I told her how funny their touch felt at first, but how nice it was, once I got used to it. She didn't say anything. I told her how gentle the people were and how there was no feel of danger or worry when they were near. Mother looked back at me and gave a heavy sigh. Still, she didn't say anything.

"I am so fed up with this," a distant voice made my ears perk. "Three times. First the dam. Then the lodge. Now the lodge again."

"Who said that?" I asked Mother.

She nodded toward the pond. "I believe it was Chippy."

We both stopped and stood a moment, listening.

"I think I'll just lie down here in the snow," the

voice said. "There's no use going on. I'm so depressed, I think I'll just give up."

Following Mother to the edge of the pond, I could see Chippy's beaver lodge out on the ice. Well—I could see what was left of it. There were limbs and dirt scattered all over the smooth white snow. Half of the lodge was open and I could see inside.

Chippy waddled into the snow and picked up a branch with his long yellow teeth. He brought it back and stuck it on his lodge. Then he turned and tapped it into place with his tail.

"Did Burly do that?" Mother called to him.

Chippy's head snapped up. He nodded to us and made a clicking sound with his teeth. "Yep. Thought with that heavy snow, the old grouch would be sound asleep. But nope! He's back again. Tearing up my lodge. Making my life miserable."

"Is there anything we can do to help?"

Chippy shook his head. "No. Not unless you know how to keep the ice open for me." He pointed with his buckteeth, toward the far end of his pond. "I can only fix part of my lodge from inside. To get most of it, I have to come out here. But if I fix my lodge, I can't get back inside. Three to five times a day I've been leaving the lodge to break the ice near the otter's den. They help, but their lodge is underground, and they don't have to keep the hole open. It's getting colder, though. Another week or so, I won't be able to . . . to . . ." He heaved another sigh and sat down on his tail. "If that old bear tears my house up again, we're goners. Thanks for your consideration, though. Got to get back to work."

"What's an otter?" I asked.

Mother motioned with a nod of her head. "On the way back from hunting our breakfast, I'll show you."

We wandered up the valley for quite a ways. Mother stopped. She heard something. Then I heard it—a faint roaring, growling sound coming from the far side of a thicket. Mother backed up. She sniffed the air. Beside us was a tall tree. I could see scratch marks in the bark. There were deep gouges—lines that reached way higher than Mother's head. She saw it, too. The snarling roar came again.

"Is that an otter?"

Mother shook her head. "No, Bub. That's Burly. It makes me nervous for you to be so close to the people. But . . ."

"Yes, Mother?"

"But for now I think we would be better off near their house. Even as nasty and mean as Burly is, I don't think he would come that close to the people."

We crossed the stream and started back. Behind us, there was more snarling and grumbling. I could hear the snapping sounds of limbs and trees breaking. It was a mean, scary sound. I was glad to be headed back. Then I heard another sound.

"Whoopieeee! Yahoooo!"
"Is that Burly?"
Mother's ears wobbled when she shook her head.
"No. Those are otters."

Chapter 1 O

"**Y**ippieee!"

"Look out! Here I come! Yahoooo!"

I wiggled my ears toward the cheers and shouts. My eyes followed where my ears led. There was a steep hill or bank not far from where Mother and I stood. It was at the opposite end of the pond from Chippy's dam. A movement at the top of the hill caught my eye.

A dark brown streak swished from the top of the rise to the bottom. It went so fast, I couldn't tell what it was. The thing didn't even slow down when it slid out onto the snow-covered pond. It just hopped up and pounced back toward the slope.

Just as it started up the hill, another brown streak swished down.

"Yippi-ty-a. Get along get along little doggie. Out of the way! Here I come!"

The second brown streak just barely missed the first. Once it hit the pond, it spun around a couple of times. But instead of hopping up and bounding back with the other one, this one just lay there—all sprawled out on its back.

"Boy, howdy. Reckon that was the best one I did all day. Look how far out on the ice I slid."

The little animal had short legs and a long tail. Instead of flat, like Chippy's tail, it was thick and tapered to a point at the end. He was lying on his back. I could see that the fur on his tummy was a lighter color.

"Look, Linda Sue. I wonder what those two big animals are."

A little head popped up, not far from where Mother and I stood.

"They're moose, you knot-head. If you'd get off your back and look at the world, right-side-up, you'd know what they were."

The little animal wiggled around and flopped over on one side. Once on his feet he stuck his pointy nose way out and looked at us. "Yep. You're right as rain, Linda Sue. They're sure enough moose."

I just knew that as little as the animal was, he would be scared of us. He'd run away and I would never know the reason for all their yelling and hollering.

Wrong.

He didn't run away. Instead, he ran right for us. His little back humped up high as he bounded through the snow, leaping and hopping his way up to where we stood. He didn't stop until he was almost standing on my hoof.

I stepped back.

He hopped closer. Sniffed. The long hairs that stuck out from either side of his mouth tickled my leg. I yanked it off the ground and held it out of his reach. He just hopped over and sniffed my other leg.

"Well, howdy, little buckaroo. You must be Bub Moose. Hey, Linda Sue. Look here. Bub Moose came to say hi."

The other little brown animal came pouncing through the snow. Standing on three legs in the deep snow was kind of awkward. Careful not to step on them, I put my foot down.

"How did you know my name was Bub?"

The otter named Linda Sue sniffed me.

"Chippy told us all about you and your mama," she answered. "He said you were about the nicest, sweetest moose that ever come down the pike. Told us you were as polite as could be."

"You know Chippy?" I had to move my feet some because they were tickling my legs with their noses again.

"Sure we know Chippy. Kid's having a mighty rough winter, what with that nasty old bear. We've been helping him keep the ice open, so he can get to the outside of his lodge. See that hole over yonder?" She pointed to a mushy spot in the ice, not far from the bank. "It's not easy, though. Hope that bear backs off soon. Pond's already froze solid. Another week and—no matter how hard we work—we won't be able to keep her open."

"He is very depressed," Mother said. "I do wish there was something we could do to help."

"Not much none of us can do, honey," Linda Sue said. "Burly is bad enough, but I reckon it's the ice that will get Chippy. Joe Bob and I knew this muskrat, one time. He wasn't too bright, but . . ."

"Ah, come on, Linda Sue, let's go slide some more. You, too, little buckaroo Bub. You can go down the slide with us."

Back arched, Joe Bob pounced across the snow. I followed him, careful not to step on Linda Sue. There in the snow was a path or trail. There were little ridges of snow on either side of it. The snow at the center was packed so tightly that it almost looked like ice. Joe Bob's long whiskers wiggled when he sniffed at the packed snow. He inched forward, then all at once he flopped on his belly.

"Yee-haaaa!" he yelped as he slid down the trough.

"Out of the way. Here I come," Linda Sue called as she leaped into the furrow. She whooshed and slid down the hill, following Joe Bob. Once at the bottom, they wrestled and tumbled over each other. Then, backs humped, they pounced to the top of their slide and took off again.

"Don't they ever get tired?" I asked Mother after we had watched them for quite a while.

Mother just smiled. "Otters have a lot of energy."

"Do they just play all the time? Don't they ever forage for food?"

"They don't eat grass and twigs, like we do, Bub. Otters eat fish. They are very fast in the water, so they have no trouble catching fish. It is so easy for them, it leaves them lots of time to play and have fun."

After about ten trips up and down their snow slide, Joe Bob and Linda Sue hopped right under my feet and looked up at me.

"Why don't you give it a shot, little Bub?"

"Yeah, it's fun, kid. Give it a try."

I looked at Mother. She shrugged. So I followed the two otters to the top of their slide. From the crest of the hill it looked like a long way to the pond. The trench where they slid was narrow and crooked. Very cautious, and a bit nervous, I stepped into the furrow.

Nothing happened.

I put my other hoof beside my first one.

"It's not working," I complained.

"You got to flop on your belly to slide down the slope. Here, watch ol' Joe Bob."

Joe Bob darted between my front legs, flopped on his tummy, and swooshed down the slope. Linda Sue nudged my hind leg with her snout.

"Go on, kid. Give it a try."

I sighed and shook my head. "I don't think it's going to work. I don't know how to flop on my tummy."

She showed me. I stretched my front hooves farther out. All they did was dig into the snow. Bounding and hopping, the two otters raced back up to me.

"How about if he sits down on his rump? Reckon that might work."

"Sure worth a try, Joe Bob."

Linda Sue stepped in front of me. She arched her back up real, real high. Then she leaned backward. Tail first, she shot down the long, windy slide.

It looked like so much fun, I just had to try it. I took a deep breath, braced myself, and folded my hind legs beneath me. Still . . .

Nothing happened. My rump just stuck there in the snow, and I didn't slide at all.

The otters raced up and down their slide. They never seemed to get tired, never seemed to slow down, and never quit their chattering and laughing. They made sliding down the slope look like *so* much fun. I really wanted to try it. But nothing I did seemed to work. Perhaps some things aren't meant to be. A moose sliding down a hill was just one of those things.

Mother told me it was time to go back down the valley. We thanked Joe Bob and Linda Sue for trying to help me.

"Think nothing of it, little Buckaroo," Joe Bob called over his shoulder as he slid down the slope again. "You'll get it next time."

Linda Sue took off after him. "Y'all come back and see us."

The hay was waiting, not far from our bed, when we got back. There were no people around. Mother and I ate our fill, then curled up together for the night.

I fell asleep with visions of skiers in my head. People laughing and giggling and zooming down the long, tall mountain. Otters flopping on their tummies and yelling and swishing down the long narrow trough. And . . . in my dreams . . . I could almost feel the rush and the excitement and the fun.

If only . . .

Chapter 11

Mother and I waited in the safety of the fir trees the next morning. The sun had been up a while before Jane and Jussy came waddling out of the barn, carrying loads of hay. Their hooves were not broad and strong like Mother's and mine. It was hard for them to walk in the deep white powder.

The people mother stood and watched. Jussy put his hay down and started back. Jane put her hay down, but instead of leaving she stood there a moment. I stepped out from behind the fir tree and started toward her.

"Bub," Mother warned. "Stay away from the people. They're dangerous."

And at the exact same second, the people mother called to her little one.

"Jane, stay away from the moose. They're dangerous."

Her little round face was pretty when she smiled and waved at me. I waved back with my ears. Once they were inside, Mother let me go eat.

Jane and Jussy came back out while we were munching the hay. They played tag around their big log cabin. People noises—laughter and giggles—filled the air. It sounded like fun. It reminded me of Snow. The little wolf and I had such a good time playing tag. I wished Snow was here. I wished I could join Jane and Jussy with their game.

Mother watched me. If I wandered toward them, she stomped a heavy hoof on the ground, warning me to come back. When Jane or Jussy moved toward us and too far from the house, the people mother told them to come back, too.

We foraged above the pond. When we strolled past it, I looked for Chippy. My friend was no place to be found. The roof of his lodge looked like it was finished. Some of the light powdery snow had blown to cover part of it, helping to keep the warmth in. Farther up the stream, we found Linda Sue and Joe Bob's slide. They weren't around, either.

There were no mean and ugly sounds from the forest. There was no prickly feeling on the back of my neck as we hunted food. Burly was not out and about this morning. I was glad. Our valley was quiet and peaceful.

Farther toward the high country, we found some green grass buried beneath the snow. While Mother ate, noises from the ski slope drew me up the far side of the ridge. Even without turning to look, I could feel Mother's eyes on me. So I didn't venture very far. I did find a place, in the middle of a tall pine grove, where I could watch. The people noises were different from the sounds the two otters made when they swished down their slide. Still, the same feeling of fun and excitement came from them. I could sense it as I watched them zoom down the hill.

Late that afternoon, as we moved toward our shelter near the people house, Joe Bob was playing on the otter slide. Linda Sue was lying on her back, munching a trout that she had caught. When she finished eating, she went to join him. Linda Sue was the one who spotted us.

"Hey, Bub," she greeted. "You come to try the slide again?"

I glanced at Mother. She smiled and shrugged her big beautiful ears. "Go ahead, if you want."

Trotting through the snow, I stopped at the very top of the otter slide. I took a deep breath and folded my legs beneath me. Nothing happened. I wiggled, trying to nestle my tummy down against the snow. I stretched my front legs out.

Still nothing.

Then I felt something on my bottom. Glancing

back, I could see Linda Sue and Joe Bob. Standing on their hind legs, they shoved and pushed with their front paws. They strained and bumped, over and over again, against my rump. I didn't budge an inch.

"Sorry, kid. It doesn't look like it's gonna work." Joe Bob sighed.

"Reckon if we rolled him over on his back?" Linda Sue suggested.

Joe Bob just shot her a disgusted look. She wiggled her whiskers and stuck her tongue out at him. Then she smiled up at me.

"Don't give up, kiddo. You'll get it—one of these days—if you keep trying."

I got to my feet, thanked them for trying to help me, then followed Mother down the valley. I wished I could ski, like the people did. I wished I could slide and play with the otters.

We returned from foraging, early that afternoon. Jane and Jussy were playing outside. I guess they were playing. Jussy was walking around, pulling on a rope. Jane sat on her bottom on some pieces of wood. There were two bright, shiny things under the wood. Wherever Jussy went with the rope, Jane and her pile of wood followed him. After a while he stopped and handed the rope to Jane.

"It's my turn to ride on the sled." Then he sat on the wood and she pulled him.

She didn't pull him very far, though. But at least she tried. Once they came sort of close to our trees.

I wanted to get a better look at the thing they called "the sled." Mother stomped her foot and snorted, telling me to stop. When the mother people saw where her little ones were, she called for them. Mother made me stay in the trees until they went back to the house.

I didn't know why Mother thought people were dangerous. I didn't know why the mother people thought moose were dangerous, either. Mother was much wiser than I was. So . . . well . . . maybe some people *were* mean—but not Jussy and *especially* not Jane. They never tried to hurt us. All they did was feed us hay. Jane was sweet and gentle. I could feel her tenderness when she had touched me. Why couldn't Mother understand? Grown-ups are so weird, sometimes.

The snowblower came the next morning. Jane and Jussy had just put our hay down and gone back to the log cabin. Mother and I hadn't even left the shelter of the trees when we heard the thing huffing and puffing up the road. Plumes of snow blew high into the air. Jane, Jussy, the people mother, and even the people daddy stood in front of their house and watched it. Holding hands in front of them, they patted them together—real fast and hard. It made a funny popping sound. Then they cheered and waved at the snowblower. I guess they were happy to see it.

★ ★ ★

It was a clear, pretty day. The sun was high—right above our heads—when Mother decided to stop searching for food and lay down. She said the winter sun was good for animals. We found a wide clearing, not far from the pond, and curled up to enjoy the wonderful day.

The snow glistened as bright as stars in the night sky. Even in a world that seemed covered with ice and snow, the sun felt warm. I closed my eyes. My head felt heavy. But before it so much as touched the snow, I heard the noise. My eyes popped wide.

The people noises were like nothing I ever heard before. There was laughter and giggles and yelling and shouting. The valley seemed to overflow with all the sounds. I stretched my neck and looked toward the pond.

There was a whole herd of people!

Beside me, I felt Mother stir. I wanted to watch and see what all the commotion was about, but I knew Mother would want to leave. Pouting, I started to get up.

"Be still, Bub." Mother nudged me with her nose. "We're far enough away. I don't think they have seen us."

The people surrounded the pond. There were seven little people—about the size of Jane and Jussy—and six big people. They carried strange things. The first thing I noticed was big and black and round. It took two of the daddy-size people to carry it. The thing reminded me of the tires on a people car, only this thing was gigantic. Two of the mother-size people carried something that looked like a leaf. It was brown and thin. Only this leaf was *enormous*. They put it down near the very top of the hill, not far from the otter slide. I saw a little blur of brown streak down the trough. Joe Bob and Linda Sue disappeared into the ice hole that they had been helping Chippy keep open. The people never saw them.

Each of the other two big people carried "the sled." Three of the Jussy-size little people carried "the sled," too. Only this "the sled" was twice as long. All the people animals climbed to the top of the hill and put their things down. Then one of the big daddy people walked out on the ice. He marched about, stomping his hooves. Then he stopped and jumped up and down.

"Frozen, solid as a rock," he called.

Everyone cheered and laughed.

The two mother-size people with the giant leaf called to the others. Everyone gathered at the back of the big leaf. They held on to one side of it as the two mother-size people climbed on. Then another big people got on with them and finally, a fourth.

"Okay!" one of them yelled. "Let it go."

The people released their hold on the back of the giant leaf. Squealing and laughing, the four mother-size people flew down the hill and way out onto

Chippy's pond. They rolled and tumbled over one another, then got to their feet and dragged it back to the top of the slope. The other two big people and three of the little people hopped on and whooshed down. When they brought it back, all the little people got on and slid.

After about five or six trips, the path that they took began to look packed and icy, just like the otter slide. They tossed the huge leaf aside and started taking turns riding "the sleds" down the slope. After they did that for a while, they got the humongous, round, black thing. Everyone sat down on it. One of the people said:

"One. Two. Three."

All at the same time they lifted their hooves and the whole bunch of them went whizzing and spinning down the slide. I never heard so much laughing and giggling and goofy sounds in my whole life.

It was almost dark when they left. They all seemed very tired and quiet. Not at all like they acted when they first got here.

Once the people were gone, Mother and I got up and started home, too.

That's when I spotted the *enormous* brown leaf. They left it behind. Right near the top of their slide.

A little shiver raced up my back, clear to my ears. Then it raced the other direction, until my tail wagged and wagged and wagged. I could hardly wait until tomorrow.

Chapter 12

Opening my eyes, I could see the bright sunshine pouring into the valley. Mother was already up. She nuzzled the snow away from the ground near the edge of the trees. Feeling safe and cozy, I wanted to sleep a little while longer.

All at once my eyes flashed wide.

The *giant* leaf!

I could hardly wait. Snow flew in all directions as I jumped up and ran to Mother.

"I'm hungry. Let's go forage up by Chippy's pond." I snuggled against her.

She glanced back at me and tilted her head, way to one side.

"Don't you want to eat first?"

"No. We don't need the people food. Let's go find our own breakfast this morning."

Mother's head tilted the other way. She studied me for a long time. Finally her ears gave a little flick.

"All right, Bub. What's going on?"

How do Mothers always know when we're up to something? I wondered. When I noticed how she looked at me—square in the eye—I knew there was no sense in trying to fib.

"I want to see if I can slide down the hill on the giant leaf."

Mother frowned and leaned both ears toward me. "Giant leaf?"

"The big, square, brown leaf that the people slid down the hill on," I explained.

Mother wobbled her head back and forth.

"That's not a leaf, Bub. It's called cardboard. It's something people make out of trees. They chew it up and smash it flat and stick it back together and . . . and well . . ." She stopped and gave a little snort. "Okay. What is it you want to do with the giant leaf?"

"I want to slide down the hill, like the people did. I couldn't go down the otter slide with Joe Bob and Linda Sue. I got stuck, remember? But I bet I can use the . . . the . . . What did you call it?"

Mother shrugged her big ears. "Giant leaf is fine."

"Yeah. I bet if I use the giant leaf, like the people did, I can slide just like the otters."

Mother looked at me a moment, then heaved a

long sigh. "All right. But if you get hurt, I'm not going to feel the least bit sorry for you."

When we got to the pond, I wanted to race across and climb the hill where the giant leaf was. Mother stomped her hoof and hrronked, calling me back to her.

"It is late enough in the winter for the pond to be safe," Mother said. "But even so, you must never go out onto the ice unless I am with you to check and make sure."

I waited while she strolled back and forth across the frozen pond. She even stopped a couple of times and pawed at spots with her big, strong hoof. Once sure it was safe, she looked at me and wobbled her ears toward the place where the giant leaf was. I charged across the pond, raced up the hill, and slid to a stop. The big brown leaf was right where the people had left it.

I leaned forward and sniffed. It didn't really smell like a leaf. I reached down and nibbled one corner. It didn't taste like a leaf. In the snow I could see tracks—webbed footprints—where the otters had come to investigate the strange thing.

Slowly and carefully I used my nose to shove it toward the edge of the slope.

"What's happenin', little buckaroo?"

The shrill, chattery voice startled me. My head was already down, shoving the leaf. I glanced between my legs. Joe Bob and Linda Sue stood right behind me.

"Did you see the people, yesterday?"

Both otters nodded. "Who could miss them. Never heard so much racket in all my days."

"Did you see them slide down the hill?"

Again they nodded.

I quit looking between my legs and stood up straight and proud. "Well, that's what I'm going to do. I'm going to use the giant leaf and slide."

Leaping and hopping over each other, Joe Bob and Linda Sue raced to me. "We'll help. What do you want us to do? Want us to give ya' a push? Just tell us what ya' want."

"I don't know yet," I told them. "Give me a second. Let me think how the people did it."

One edge of the giant leaf was hanging over the crest of the slope. I studied it a moment, trying to remember. Okay—they got on the leaf and sat down. I looked at it and nibbled my bottom lip. I can do that. I know how to fold my hind legs under me and sit down. Yeah . . . I can do that.

My eyes flashed. *Wait. There's something else.*

"I know how you can help," I told the otters. "Part of the people held the leaf, while the others sat down on it. Will you hold it for me?"

"Sure thing, little buckaroo." Joe Bob pounced up to the edge of the leaf. He took one corner in his teeth and bit down. Linda Sue raced to the other corner and chomped down on it.

"Wegoter, iddleBub. Annetyme yourready," they mumbled.

It was really hard to understand them, since they had to talk out of one side of their mouths, while holding the giant leaf in their teeth.

I took a deep breath. Left front hoof, then right front hoof. Left rear hoof, then right rear hoof. Walk to the middle and sit down. I got it now. I can do it. Here goes.

I put my left front hoof on the leaf. Then I put my right front hoof on the leaf. Then . . .

The leaf took off!

I wasn't ready. I only had my front hooves on the thing.

The leaf didn't care. It just *whooshed* away, down the steep hill. Since my front hooves were on it—they went, too. Only my back hooves were still stuck in the snow. I didn't even have time to jump back. There was a little *whoomp* sound. It came from me when my tummy hit the ground.

Then . . . away I went.

I guess I should say—away we went. Joe Bob and Linda Sue were still clamped on to their corners of the leaf. Stretched out on our tummies, all three of us went zooming down the hill.

Sprawled flat, my front hooves and chest were on

the giant leaf. Hind legs and tummy floundered about, chasing the rest of me and the leaf down the steep slope. I was going *really* fast. Then faster and faster and . . .

The wind fluttered my eyelashes. It whistled in my ears.

Faster. Faster!

Everything happened so quickly, I didn't even know what was going on until we slowed at the far side of the pond. When we finally stopped, I lay there a moment. I was still holding my breath. When I let it out, this strange sound came out of me. It was a laugh. Not a people laugh, but a moose laugh.

I laughed and laughed and laughed until a little tear came to my eye.

"Yee-haaaa!" Joe Bob yelped, once he let go of the leaf.

"Yahoooo!" Linda Sue squealed. She hopped over my back and went to wrestle with Joe Bob. "What a ride, cowboy. We went clean to the far bank of the pond. Reckon that's the best slide that we ever had."

They laughed and tumbled and played. I had to stop for a second to catch my breath. Mother stood high on the slope of the valley. Frozen, she watched until she was sure I was okay. Then she shook her head, rolled her eyes, and went back to munching on the green fir boughs.

I had to roll over on one side and tuck my legs

under me to get up. As soon as I was on my feet, I heard a sound. It was weird. Sort of a yapping, howling, snorting noise—all rolled into one.

I looked up the hill where we just came from. At first I couldn't see what was making all the racket. Then I saw three black dots in the solid white. Two black eyes and a black nose.

"Snow!" I hrronked. "Snow? It that you?"

The white wolf howled and hooted. He flopped around in the snow, rolling from side to side, like he was having a fit or something. It had been so long since I had seen Snow. I charged across the pond and galloped up the hill.

He didn't even look up. He just kept rolling and laughing his fool tail off. "That's the funniest thing I ever saw in my life," he howled. "You should have seen your eyes. I didn't know moose's eyes could get that big around. I mean . . . there you went . . . sprawled out flat on your belly . . . flying down the hill. And the two otter . . . hanging on . . . bouncing around, right there with you." He started howling and rolling in the snow again. I walked over to him and gave him a big wet kiss.

"Hey, what's that all about?" Snow shook his fur and shot me a disgusted look.

"I'm so happy to see you. What are you doing here?"

"My pack is just passing through. We've been down, hunting rabbits. Headed back up to the high

country. We'll just be here a day or two. But I never expected to see . . . to see—" he broke off, howling again. "Never expected to see a moose go flying down a hill like that."

"It was fun!" I puffed out my chest and stood tall. "You ought to try it."

Snow shook his head.

I raised an eyebrow. "What's wrong? You scared?"

That was all it took. We spent the rest of the afternoon taking turns sliding down the hill on the giant leaf. Getting it to the top was easy, once Snow got in on things. He latched on to one corner and, growling and snarling, tugged the thing to the top.

I asked him if all that noise was really necessary. He just wagged his tail and told me that it helped.

Once Joe Bob and Linda Sue found that Snow was no threat to them, they even joined in.

I would hold the leaf down with my hoof while Snow and the two otters climbed on. As soon as they were ready, I raised my hoof and off they went. Snow would drag the leaf back to the top. There, he and the otters would hold it while I got on.

Sometimes I got on. Most times it started sliding. Snow, Joe Bob, and Linda Sue just weren't heavy enough to hold me. So all four of us would go flying down the hill, sprawled out on our bellies. I never had so much fun.

We were just preparing to make another run when

suddenly Snow froze. Eyes tight, he looked toward a pine thicket not far from Chippy's dam.

"What is it?" I whispered.

Snow's lip curled on one side. He let out a little growl. "People. There by the trees. People are the most dangerous animal in the forest."

Stretching my neck toward the pines, I finally spotted what Snow was talking about. Jane and Jussy stood there, watching us. They pointed and giggled and laughed.

"Those aren't people," I told Snow. "Those are Jane and Jussy."

Snow's sharp little pointy ears perked. "Not people?"

"Well, okay—they're people. But they're nice people. They won't hurt us. Come on. Let's slide some more."

Still keeping one eye on Jane and Jussy, Snow latched on to the edge of the giant leaf. I raised my foot to step on it. But before I could put it down . . .

The sound of crashing limbs and brush came to our ears. Eyes wide, all of us spun to look at the trees where the two little people were.

"Grrr . . . ow! Grrr . . . ow!"

"Run!" Snow's yap was shrill and high. "It's Burly! He almost got my dad yesterday." Snow took off for the far ridge. *"Run!"*

Jussy and Jane must have heard the sound before we did. Both scrambled for the nearest pine and climbed as fast as they could. Jussy just barely got his legs out of the way when the huge grizzly bear skidded into the branches at the bottom of their tree. Growling and snarling, Burly stood up on his back legs and slapped at the boy above him.

Jane screamed as she scrambled higher. Burly tried to climb up, but the fat old bear was too heavy for the small tree. Sitting on his haunches, he grabbed the pinc with his front paws and shook it as hard as he could.

"He-e-e-lp!" Jussy screamed. His legs dangled down, just inches from Burly's reach.

Burly roared and snarled. He was huge. I'd never seen an animal so big. Jane cried.

She was so tiny. So helpless as she clung to the pine limb, just above the enormous, nasty old bear.

Chapter 13

Growling and snarling, Burly slapped at the dangling legs. Branches cracked. Pine needles flew through the air. Just at the last second Jussy tucked his knees up, out of Burly's reach. Eyes big, he used every bit of strength to pull himself higher in the small pine and away from those long sharp claws.

Burly was big—no, he was *huge*. He was mean and nasty. I could just barely see Jane's bright fur, up high in the pine tree. But I could hear her cries and whimpers. Jane was little and sweet. She was always nice to me and Mother. She never, ever hurt us. All she did was feed us hay. She was so tiny and Burly was so big and . . .

The huge bear took another swing at Jussy's dangling legs. Once more he managed to pull them out of reach. Jussy fed me hay, too. He left the giant leaf,

106

here by the pond, so I could slide and play and . . . and . . .

Snarling and snapping, Burly grabbed the trunk of the little tree and shook it again.

I felt my eyes squint. The muscles in my shoulders and legs drew up tight and hard. This wasn't right! The two little people animals were sweet and gentle. They never did anything to that nasty old bear. It just wasn't right for him to try and hurt them.

I charged! My feet dug the snow. Puffs of white powder flew toward the sky. Hard and fast as I could, I raced toward the ferocious beast. At the last second I lowered my head and rammed the mean monster—right on his furry, hairy bottom.

"Hhurrmph!"

I don't know what I expected. I guess I thought my mighty charge would send Burly tumbling away from the trees and away from Jane and Jussy. I didn't want to hurt him, I just wanted him to leave the little people alone. He was supposed to get up, dust his fur off, and then run away.

Only when I hit him the big bear didn't budge. I did.

My head hurt. Things kind of spun around as I bounced backward and went, *kerplop* into a snowbank on my rump. I blinked a couple of times to get my eyes to stop rolling around in my head.

Ever so slowly—like he was looking for nothing

more than a mosquito that landed on his fur—Burly turned.

"Oh, a moose. So you think you can take on Burly Bear, do you?" His eyes narrowed to tiny slits.

"The little people animals are my friends." I tried to sound brave and strong as I struggled to pull my rump out of the snowbank. "Why are you mad at them? They didn't do anything to you. Leave them alone!"

When Burly just looked at me and licked his lips, I knew I was a goner. He lunged. I didn't have time to run. I didn't have time to dodge out of his way. Only his feet slipped in the snow. Even at that, he would have still gotten me if his shoulder hadn't bumped against the pine tree trunk.

Crack! Snap!

Branches broke. Then more bent and crunched as the little boy people lost his grip and fell from the tree. Burly only took a step or two toward me when he heard the noise behind him. He spun around, just in time to see Jussy land, with a thud, in the soft snow.

The second he turned toward the boy, I lowered my head and rammed him again. This time, as soon as I butted him, I wheeled around and took off running. "Look out, Moosie!" Jane screamed from the pine tree. "He's going to get you. Justin, hurry. Climb back up the tree!"

"I'll get you, Moose!" Burly snarled. He was so

close, I could almost feel his hot breath on the back of my legs. I ran harder. Burly growled. He was really mad now. I was in so much trouble . . .

"*Mommieeeee!*" I hrronked. "*Help!*"

"It's too late for your mommy to save you," Burly snarled at my heels. "You're nothing but lunch now."

Running as hard as I could, I managed to stay just ahead of the nasty old bear. Then suddenly the snow beneath my feet felt different. I couldn't get hold of it. I couldn't run. All I could do was slip.

My legs locked, but I still kept moving. I slid. Then I spun sideways. Then . . . I was going round and round and round. I slowed to a stop, just in time to see Burly come sliding past me. Flat on his belly, with all four legs sprawled out, he swished right on by and plowed into the snowbank on the far side of the pond.

It took him a second to pull his head out of the white powder.

I tried to turn and run back toward the pine trees, only nothing happened. My feet spun and churned on the slippery ice, but I didn't go anyplace. Burly came toward me, once more. Only this time he didn't run. He took one slow step at a time. I tried harder to run away. Even running as fast as my legs would go, I still didn't get anyplace.

Closer and closer, Burly closed the distance between us. He reared up on his hind legs. Slobbers dripped from his mouth. I trembled. He raised his huge paw. Sharp claws glistened. Then . . .

Burly's eyes flashed. He opened his enormous mouth, as if he were going to let out his horrible roar.

Instead . . . nothing came out but a little squeak.

Confused, I tilted my head to one side. Burly squeaked again, then wheeled around. When he spun away from me, I saw this ball of white fur attached to his rump.

It was Snow!

Snarling and growling, the little white wolf dug his teeth into Burly's backside.

"Run, Bub," he mumbled. (It was hard to understand him because of all the bear fuzz he had clamped between his teeth.) "I got him. Run!"

Burly turned his head to bite Snow. Only when he turned his head, his back end turned, too. Snow was just out of reach when the bear's enormous jaws snapped shut. Burly whipped around the other direction. Again those sharp, nasty teeth just missed the little wolf.

Burly reached back with his paw. I heard a little whimper as I saw Snow flying across the pond.

Eyes tight and black as death, the huge bear turned back to me. I stared him square in the eye. No matter how mean and brave I tried to look—it didn't work. I was scared.

The ice seemed to shake beneath my hooves. I

blinked and yanked my eyes away from Burly. Behind him there was a movement. Something big and brown and fast came flying down the bank and across the pond.

"Leave my baby alone!" Mother hrronked.

Almost before I even realized that it was her, Mother crashed into Burly.

All three of us went whirling and spinning and sliding across the ice. We didn't stop until we crashed into this pile of snow-covered logs and sticks. In a heap we landed tangled up against the big mound of limbs. I was on the bottom, Mother was on top of me, and Burly was . . .

"Get off," a strange little voice mumbled. Something wiggled beneath me.

"What?"

"Get off," it mumbled again. "You're smushing me."

It was Snow. I jerked and struggled, trying to get to my feet. Mother lunged and strained, trying to get off me. It was no use. We were so tangled with the logs and branches and with one another, we could hardly move.

Slowly Burly wallowed to his feet. He licked his lips and smiled.

"I'm in for a great meal. Two moose, a wolf, then when I finish up, there's the two little people and—"

"I've had about enough of this! All winter long, it's the same old stuff. Knock my dam apart. Tear up my lodge. Stupid bear is supposed to be sleeping, and he just won't leave us alone. I'll probably end up as a beaver hat, but . . . *I'm not taking this anymore!*"

The voice came from behind the pile of brush. Two furry faces, with long buckteeth, popped out and glared at Burly.

"Me, neither! *Let's get him!*"

Chippy hopped over what was left of his beaver lodge and latched on to Burly's little stub tail.

"Grrr . . . yelp!" Burly slapped at Chippy.

He finally hit him and sent him sailing across the ice. As soon as he did, Chippy's wife hopped up and chomped down on his little stub tail. Burly howled again. He knocked her off, too, but the moment he did, Chippy came hopping and bounding across the ice, made a flying leap, and latched on to that tail again. Then Joe Bob came flying across the ice and latched on to the little toe on the bear's left foot. Linda Sue got hold of his right ankle.

The big bear shifted from one foot to the other, trying to make the mad beavers and the ferocious otters stop nipping at him. Snow managed to wiggle out from under me. He got to his feet and bit the bear on his other leg, then hopped back out of reach.

A rock flew through the air and clunked Burly on the head. Then another rock came flying. Then there were sticks and stones and . . .

"Justin, you get back up that tree, where it's safe!"

The people mother stood on the pond bank, throwing everything she could get her hands on at the nasty old bear. Jussy didn't mind his mother. He stood right next to her, throwing rocks and limbs at Burly as fast as he could throw.

Mother struggled to her feet. She pawed the snow and ice. She lowered her head at Burly and hrronked. I hopped up and stood bravely beside her.

"Go on, get away from us," I hrronked.

"Yip, yip, yap, yap! Snow howled between nips at the old bear.

Another rock clunked Burly on the head.

Burly suddenly stood up. Eyes crossed, he blinked a couple of times and looked around. A beaver's buckteeth were sunk into his tail, a white wolf leaped in and bit, then hopped out of the way. Another beaver and two otters bounded and pounced back across the pond toward the action. More rocks and branches flew through the air from the people on the bank. And a mother moose and a baby moose lowered their heads to charge.

In the blink of an eye the big bear whirled around and raced toward the far side of the pond.

Chippy dropped from Burly's rear end at the edge of the ice. The big beaver puffed up his fur and stood, staring at the escaping bear. As soon as he let go and waddled back toward his lodge and the rest of us, two wolves appeared from the trees. They charged after Burly, nipping and biting at his heels with every step he took.

Chippy slapped his flat tail down on the ice.

"And let that be a lesson to you, you big . . .you big ball of stinky bear fuzz! Come around here again and we'll gnaw you into little pieces!" Chippy's wife looked very proud as she watched her husband.

"Yeah, if you ever show your stinkin' hide round here, again, the whole bunch of us'll have bear stew for supper." Joe Bob brushed his front paws together and spat in the snow.

As Burly disappeared into the edge of the trees, we could hear him mumble.

"I've never seen such a crazy place. No wonder I can't get any sleep. First off, the people come in and build a ski lodge over my den. Then I'm attacked by a baby moose and a baby wolf. They're supposed to be afraid of bears . . . not attack them. Even the people don't run away, like they normally do. They start throwing rocks. A Mama moose tries to run over me. Then . . . on top of all that . . . two stinking little beavers start gnawing on my tail like it's a willow tree. And a couple of otters try to chew my toes off. That's it! I've had it! I'm out of here!"

Snow's mother and father nipped at his heels as he ran. "And don't come back, either!" they howled.

Everyone watched the far mountainside. At last we saw Burly's huge, lumbering form as he broke from the trees and raced across the white, snow-covered clearing—one of the wolves still chasing him. Snow's mother trotted across the frozen pond and stood next to her son. She sniffed him all over, to make sure he was all right, then she stood to watch.

The huge, nasty, scary, old bear was nothing more than a brown speck by the time he finally disappeared over the crest of the mountain.

As Burly vanished—forever—Snow's daddy came trotting out of the trees. "Sorry we were so late getting here, Snow. Your mom and I came as quick as we could. I guess you were doing okay, though. You guys had things under control and didn't even need . . ."

He stopped talking. His eyes popped open big and his mouth gaped.

Head tilted to one side, I couldn't help but wonder what he was staring at. I looked around.

Jussy and Jane stood right next to me. Their mother was right behind them. My mother and Snow's mother stood on my other side. Snow was so close, he was practically under my hooves. In front of us, Joe Bob and Linda Sue watched as Chippy and his wife began to rebuild their lodge.

When Mother looked around, her eyes got big and her ears stood straight up. I guess she didn't realize she was standing so close to the people and the wolves. Jane and Justin's mom's eyes flashed wide,

too. The breath kind of caught in her throat, and she made a strange sound when she swallowed.

One slow, cautious step at a time the Mothers backed away. Snow's mother went to the far side of the pond and stood next to Snow's father. My mother moved to the edge of the trees. The people mother, holding Jane and Jussy by the hands, moved toward the safety of the pines.

No one said a word.

For a long time all three of our mothers watched. The people mother finally broke the silence. Her smile was gentle when she cupped a hand beside her mouth.

"Thank you," she called.

Snow's mother wagged her tail. My mother wobbled her ears and nodded. Each looked at the other. Quietly shaking their heads—they all walked away.

I looked down at Snow. "Want to play on the slide again?"

He flipped his tail. Then, with a little glint in his eye, he jumped up and hit me on the rump with his paws.

"Tag. You're it."

About the Authors

CAROL WALLACE and **BILL WALLACE** finished this story on the day they celebrated their thirty-fifth wedding anniversary. Parents of three children, they live on a farm in southwest Oklahoma—the last place anyone would go to find a moose.

But if one were to go to the neighbor's house—a short walk across the pasture—Nikki, Carol and Bill's daughter, will be more than happy to show her collection. Also a published author, Nikki has been finding moose for over fifteen years. (Some she even found in Oklahoma.)

Both former educators, Bill was principal and P.E. teacher at the same school he attended as a child. Carol taught second grade for twenty-six years. She now writes full-time, travels, and speaks with her husband at schools and conferences.